THE MERMAID

By Shane Scollins

THE MERMAID

Limitless Publishing, LLC
Kailua, HI 96734
www.limitlesspublishing.com

Formatting: Limitless Publishing

ISBN-13: 978-1-64034-154-8
ISBN-10: 1-64034-154-4

Dedication

This book is dedicated to the dreamers, the believers...those that see magic in the world and refuse to let it die.

The sea, once it casts its spell,
Holds on in its net of wonder forever.

~Jacques Yves Cousteau

Chapter 1

Jake

Every night for three weeks, it's been the same routine, with the same outcome. He puts the gun to his head, and he fails to pull the trigger. The worst part is he can't even understand why his finger betrays him. The wick has burned, the trigger is light, the grip is firm, the gun feels right.

His mind was never going to set him free. Being a prisoner of your own self-inflicted anguish is exhausting to the point of demise. The untimely end is all that seems fitting. Yet this exercise in futility itself has become cumbersome.

It was impossible to forget the sounds of screeching tires, crunching steel, and shattering glass. But the worst sounds were the moans of agony issuing from the human bodies that endured the chaos. No matter how hard he tried, he wasn't getting the sounds and images out of his head without the help of the memory-cleansing bullet from the dark chamber of this pistol.

1

Jake had second-guessed himself about a thousand times since that night. There was no way around it, the fault rested squarely on his shoulders. The frayed rope of his sanity had unraveled. He'd run out of time, energy, and money. It was time to get this over and done with.

This was Cassie's favorite place in the world, the large stones that formed the breakers at Fort Fisher. After leaving the beach, she'd always wanted to come here and climb the large rocks. Jake always tried to discourage her, not because of the large signs that said, *'Keep Off,'* but because it was dangerous. There were large gaps one could slip into and easily break an ankle, sprain a knee, or worse.

That ironic fact was not lost on him. Jake had always been the smart one, the safe one. He didn't take stupid chances or put himself in danger. At least not since he was a teen, which is what made his actions that night even harder to understand.

There was no point thinking anymore. He was done. His brain was just too tired, too worn down. This was a fight he no longer wanted, a battle of attrition with no winner.

Just like the previous nights, he slid the pistol out of his pocket and glared at it in his hand. The black weapon looked menacing just sitting still. The lethal power was resting silently in the chamber, a twitch of his finger away from killing him. It seemed so easy to access. But easy was never simple.

Tears formed in his eyes and slid down his cheeks. If Cassie could see him now she'd cry too, she'd beg him not to do it, not to end it. But he just couldn't take the pain anymore, it was too hard. The loneliness was so palpable it shook him in fits of cold shiver. He'd loved Cassie with every bit of his soul and he knew in his heart he'd never find that again. Life was not worth living without her and that was that.

He looked at the nearly full moon. Swallowed his tears behind a spray of seawater and put the gun to his temple. The finger on his right hand would not betray him tonight. It was happening and he didn't have the will to stop himself this time.

With his finger pressed to the trigger, he screamed at the moon, into the night. A soft squeeze didn't get it done, and he was about to do what he'd failed to do so many times before. In that brief silence before death, a soft voice said, "Please no, please stop!"

Jake let up and blinked away the tears. He searched around for the source of the voice, looked down. At the edge of the rocks, lapped by waves and touched by the moon's light, he saw a beautiful blonde girl in the surf.

He couldn't find a single word. He could see her clearly enough to see the sparkle in her eyes and the apple cheekbones. Was this even real? Had he already pulled the trigger?

Then he managed to utter a raspy, "Hello?"

She didn't reply with words, only a smile, the sweetest smile he'd ever seen. But when he stood up and saw her entire form, his jaw fell open, wordless.

Her smile quickly faded and a look of panic struck her. In one move, she dove off the rocks and into the water. With one swift flip, she was gone.

Jake stood there; he didn't even realize at some point he'd dropped the pistol into one of the deep fissures between the huge boulders. But what he'd just seen was something he could not explain. And even if he could explain it, he couldn't possibly tell anyone about it without sounding like a psychotic.

He slumped back onto the rock and looked across the waves. There she was again, bobbing out in the breakers like a surfer waiting for a set.

Jake started down the rocks, running toward the sand of the nearby beach to his right. He chugged over to the loose soil and saw her. He wanted to yell or something, but no sounds formed for his tongue to sculpt. Instead, he stuck his arm up to wave. After a brief moment, she sank under the sea and was gone.

Jake was unable to move for several seconds, or perhaps it was minutes, or even hours. Time ceased to exist. Finally, he decided it was time to get back to reality with a long shake of his head.

After an extensive search for the gun, he was unable to find it. That was bothersome because he worried it would end up in the wrong hands. In the morning, he'd come back and return to the search effort.

Right now, he just sat in his car trying to understand what he'd seen. With his phone in hand, he started doing some searches for mermaids. He knew they weren't real, or at least he'd never believed they were. They were a child's fantasy, certainly not a real thing.

Maybe his eyes had deceived him. Maybe there

was never anything there at all. If his body had released some sort of pre-death hormone that caused him to hallucinate, he'd believe that more than the fact he'd just seen a mermaid.

With nothing left to think, and no gun with which to blow his brains out, he started his car and headed home.

Chapter 2

Sleep didn't come easy. He'd spent the entire night tossing and turning as usual. But there was one significant difference. He didn't spend the night thinking about Cassie and the accident. Instead, he spent the night thinking of the girl on the rocks, the mermaid.

He wondered who she was. It was more likely that she was not a real mermaid even if she was real. He'd seen those girls that train professionally for shows; they had very convincing costumes and practiced for years to be fluid in the water.

He laughed at himself as he kicked his feet off the bed to the floor. He stood in front of the bathroom mirror and laughed again. On the bright side, he hadn't laughed in months. He was clearly cracking up with insanity.

After climbing into a black t-shirt and some blue board shorts, he headed down the hallway. In the living room on the dingy mocha-colored couch, his roommate Tom sat, eating a giant bowl of Honey Nut Cheerios.

"Morning," Jake said as he opened the fridge.

With his mouth half full, Tom replied, "Did I just hear you laughing?"

"Yeah. Yeah, you did."

Tom didn't look up from the cereal bowl. "That's different."

Jake cracked open a bottled iced coffee drink and took a long swig. "Yeah, it was a different night." He swung the door of the old fridge, covered in stickers, closed.

Tom slurped from his spoon. "What time did you get home?"

"Around one-thirty."

"Wanna go out today? The boards are waxed and that hurricane in the South-A is stirring up some killer sets. Gonna be going off all week."

Jake sneered at him. "You've asked me every day for four months if I want to go surfing. I haven't gone once. Why do you keep asking?"

"Faith, bruh, faith."

"Faith in what?"

"In the sea...in humanity."

"Humanity?"

Tom turned to look at him briefly, his shaggy blond hair in his face. "You are human, aren't you?"

Jake shrugged. "I guess so."

"So you'll get over this tragedy and be back to yourself eventually. We all do."

"That's optimistic."

"No, that's faith, bruh. Time deals all pain a complex hand...doesn't make it gone, just makes it easier to live with, my friend."

Jake nodded thoughtfully. Tom was a very sage-like guy and often had nothing interesting to say for days at a time. But then he'd spout off something that you just had to listen to and think about. His shaggy blond hair and sculpted tan body screamed prototypical surfer and beach bum. That is exactly what he was.

"Hey, Tom, let me ask you something. What do you know about mermaids?"

Tom didn't glance up. Instead he tipped the bowl to his mouth and drank the milk from the bottom with a sip. After draining the contents, he burped and then stood. "Mermaids? You mean those little surf babes that hang out at the pier?" He shrugged. "I mean, they're cute, but way too young."

"No, that's not what I'm talking about. I'm talking about real mermaids, the mythical ones."

Tom scrunched his face. "I don't know, man. Why're you asking about mermaids?"

"Just curious. Do you think something like that could be real?"

Tom moved into the kitchen and placed his bowl in the sink. "I think there's a lot of stuff in the world science can't explain."

"But you believe in UFOs and Bigfoot, the Loch Ness Monster and all that stuff."

"Sure I do."

"So what about mermaids?"

Tom shrugged. "I dunno, man. I've spent a lot of time in the water. I think I'd've seen one by now. I mean, if I'd spent as much time in Loch Ness as I have the ocean, I bet I'd've seen the monster by now. Shit, we'd probably be buds by now. He'd like

8

come up and I'd like scratch his belly and shit."

Jake nodded. "That's fair."

Tom took hold of an apple from the bowl on the counter. "Why the sudden interest in mermaids? Did you see one?" He chuckled.

Jake just shook his head. "No, man, just thinking about stuff."

"Well, ponder away. I'm heading out to catch waves. If you're ready to stop being a capo, you know you're welcome to tag."

"What beach?"

"Going up to Wrightsville to meet Megan. She texted me last night and said it's going off up top."

"What's the deal with you two? You've been together like every day for the past three months."

Tom took a few steps down the hallway and stopped. "Hadn't really thought about it. She's a cool chick with a hot body who likes to cut waves. Why does there have to be a deal?" He continued down the hallway and closed his bedroom door behind him.

Jake didn't really have an agenda today. The fact he wasn't dead was about all the excitement he could handle. For the first time in months, he wanted to do something other than mope around the house and wait for nightfall so he could blow his brains out. So that was different.

After putting on some blue Nike sneakers, he grabbed his keys and headed out to his old-ish, faded red Volkswagen Beetle. The car started and drove well, but it looked like it was getting tired. It had well over one hundred thousand miles and probably needed about a thousand dollars in work to get it back up to full operating order. But he didn't care. He didn't get much money from his insurance company to replace his car and this was all he could afford. Plus he didn't want anything nice ever again.

After he stopped going to work, he burned through his savings, mostly on alcohol. But his original plan was to just kill himself once he was out of money. He'd been out of money now for a few weeks. A visit to the pawnshop to sell some of the jewelry he'd gotten for Cassie had given him enough to get by for a while.

He'd gotten her a few nice pieces for the wedding, a gift to wear as she walked down the aisle. She'd never gotten the chance to wear any of it.

Selling her jewelry made him feel like garbage. It was just one more nail in his coffin that he didn't really need. But in the end he decided there was no point in leaving it to anyone else. There was no one really to leave it to, anyway. It's not like he was going to leave it to his parents. They didn't really need money, and they never graced him with any siblings.

After a few moments of contemplation, he finally started the car and headed toward Fort Fisher. He wanted to find that gun before anyone else did.

The roads swam under his car. He didn't really drive down them anymore. He used to love driving. It was one of his favorite things. Whenever he and his friends went out, he'd always driven. He'd rather have driven and let them all drink than trust anyone else behind the wheel.

As he passed by the road that led to the intersection of that fateful moment, he couldn't stop the tears from welling up in his eyes. He'd cried more in the past year than he had in his entire life. The pain was not really receding as the experts indicated it would.

Time heals all wounds, or so they say. But so far time wasn't even making a dent in his agony. It was constant and he just felt like it wasn't going to get any better. Ever.

Wheeling into the parking lot, he shut off the engine and got out. The summer sun was at midmorning position, hanging over the ocean and cooking the landscape. It was going to be a hot North Carolina summer day.

After surveying the scene, a few cars parked in the lot to his left, he strode toward the rocks and stepped up on the first one, carefully navigating his way up to the top above the water. To his right people on the small cove beach scampered. He took no joy in their playfulness. In fact, he hated them.

A few surfers bobbed out in the waves, he hated them too. He hated everything and everyone. But he didn't want some kid to find that gun so he started searching.

Chapter 3

The afternoon sped by with incredible rapidity and his search for the missing pistol had come up empty. It was probably time to just give up and resign himself to the fact that some kid had found it, and was probably going to accidentally kill his baby sister while they ate their breakfast. The only hope he had was to pray that his luck did not turn into anyone else's bad luck.

He slumped down and sat on one of the flat rocks, letting his feet dangle over the softly spraying surf below. Though he didn't want to, he kept thinking about what happened last night. At the risk of going insane, he wanted to see the girl in the water again. Simultaneously, he thought that if he'd found that gun, tonight would finally be the night.

Clearly, he was losing his mind anyway, there was no reason to stick around and go crazy. It would be a step too far to suffer the indignity of ending up in a psych hospital jacked full of Geodon and Seroquel.

Seeing mermaids was the last straw. He just

wanted to fall into the water and drown himself. If he thought it would work he'd do it in a second. But he was a good swimmer and he wasn't convinced he'd be able to let himself drown. The instinct to live would probably kick in and save him.

He realized he hadn't eaten all day when his stomach started growling. He was so hungry he began to feel sick, and when he stood up, a dizzy spell hit him. Quickly he sat back down so he didn't tumble into the water.

Just as he caught his breath, she said, "Careful, you don't want to fall."

He looked down when he heard her voice, and there she was again, the blonde girl with her elbows leaning on the wooden pylon below the rocks and her bottom half somewhere below the black waters.

He had no words. He was afraid to speak anything for fear she might go away…or maybe that she wouldn't.

"Don't you have anything to say?"

It was clear she was not a regular girl in a mermaid costume. He didn't know how he knew that, but it was obvious. Softly, he made a word. "You."

"Yes, me."

"Who are you?"

"I am Ariel."

"Ariel?" He laughed. "Seriously?"

"Why is that odd?"

"The mermaid from the cartoon?"

"I don't know what you mean."

Jake laughed and raised his arms in a V. "What the hell is this? Thank you. I'm going insane. Am I on some sort of hidden camera show?"

Ariel moved a little to his left. "I don't know what you mean with any of this."

"Who are you?"

"I told you who I am."

Jake looked at her in the moonlight. She was beautiful, just stunning. His imagination was excellent. "Okay, I'll play along. Why not? I'm already insane. I mean, clearly." He raised his arms again and yelled, "Clearly insane!"

"Are you insane?"

"You tell me." He gestured to the sea.

"I wouldn't know. I don't know you well enough."

Jake snickered awkwardly. "Of course not, you're a figment of my own imagination. Why would you know me?"

"Do you not think I'm real?"

"Of course you're not real. I'm insane. I'm talking to a mermaid and I'm insane!" He yelled louder, "I'm talking to a mermaid and I'm insane."

"Who are you yelling to? There's no one around."

"I don't know. Maybe God! Maybe Poseidon!" He smacked his hands into his thighs. "How could you be real?" Jake moved down a few rocks to get closer.

Ariel moved away almost instinctively. "I'm as real as you are."

Jake moved down another couple of rocks. "Maybe I'm not real. Maybe I'm already dead. Maybe I didn't drop the gun last night, maybe I pulled the trigger."

14

She moved away again. "Do you want to be dead?"

"I've been trying to get there."

"I know. I've been watching you."

Jake stopped in his tracks and locked in on her eyes. They were the bluest pair of eyes he'd ever seen. Even in this low light of the moon, the crystal blue was stunning. They were not that different from the blue tone of his but they were lighter and had more depth. "You've been watching me? Why?"

"You were a curious one to watch. You're not like the others. I've watched you cry many nights. I heard you singing a sad song." She looked away, then met his eyes more directly. "I saw you with the gun to your head."

He leaned back. "I don't know what to say."

"You don't have to say anything."

"Why didn't you talk to me before?"

She shrugged. "Because last night was the first time you were actually going to do it."

"Really? How did you know?"

She pushed away from the rocks and began to tread water. "I had a feeling."

"Do you have, like, psychic powers or something?"

Ariel chuckled. "No, silly, I don't think so." She became more serious. "I can tell when someone else is in pain."

Jake stepped slowly down another few rocks. She kept her distance and he didn't want to spook her. "Why is this happening to me?"

"Why is what happening?"

"Oh, I don't know. I'm sitting on the rocks talking to a mermaid. No, it's not strange at all. This happens to me all the time."

She moved back and kicked some water up at him. "There's no need for the sarcasm."

Jake flinched from the water as it fell short of hitting him. "I think this is *my* hallucination, so the sarcasm is warranted."

"What will it take to convince you I'm real?"

"I don't know."

"Ask me anything."

He thought for a second. "Can anyone else see you?"

"They can, but I prefer they don't."

"Why?"

"Why do you think?"

Jake looked around. There were a few people way down on the beach to his right fishing with some lights on their caps, but other than that no one was close enough to see him in the growing darkness. "I can imagine all people might not be so nice."

She smiled uncomfortably. "I'm a spectacle."

He looked at her. "Can I ask you questions?"

She shrugged. "I just said you can ask me anything you want."

"Where do you live?"

Ariel swam in a circle. "I have a home."

"Do you live alone?"

"No."

"Who do you live with?"

"Father."

"How old are you?"

16

"Old enough."

"Are there others like you?"

She shook her head. "I'm the only one."

"Wait, I'm confused. If you're the only one, how were you born?"

Ariel floated on her back away from the shore. "I have to go now."

Jake stood up. "Wait, don't go yet."

"I'm sorry, it's time to go."

"Will I see you again?"

"Come tomorrow, at sundown." She sank under the surface and disappeared with a bloop.

Chapter 4

Exploring the disheveled roadside shop, Jake wasn't looking for anything in particular. He was really just wasting hours until it was time to head to the beach. The next mermaid encounter was all that was on his mind, but he'd always wanted to come into this place. He'd driven by it a hundred times, in fact he used to play baseball on the field right down the street. Yet, he'd never ventured into the place. His mother always told him it was a dirty place and never to go in there. His mother was always worried about dirty things and germs. Even though he was long into adulthood, sometimes things your parents said carried with you.

Jake assumed the longer he went without seeing the mermaid the more it would seem like an illusion. But oddly the opposite was happening. It seemed more real as time wore on. The longer it had to sink in, the more viable it seemed.

All the odd trinkets on the shelves were tourist-friendly. Jake imagined that this place raked in the cash during the holiday weekends. The beaches of

North Carolina were magnets for everyone this side of the Mississippi river. If you didn't want to drive all the way to Florida, North Carolina was the best beach state on the east coast.

Just as he put down a plastic turtle, he heard his name.

"Jake?"

He turned and saw her walking toward him. She wore a blue blouse and white shorts. Her long brown hair rested in a loose ponytail draped over her left shoulder, and her big brown eyes were smiling as they always had.

He found his voice. "Ashley? Oh wow, hey."

"How've you been, Jake?" She gave him a short hug and pulled back. "I heard you moved away."

"Who said I moved?"

"I ran into Pete and Roxy a few weeks ago at The Cantina. They said you sold the store and moved to New York."

He shook his head. "No, I didn't."

"Are you planning on it?"

He shrugged a little. "I thought about it for about a minute, but it was never an option."

"Where're you living? I drove by the house and it's still empty. It's up for sale."

Jake swallowed hard, biting his lip. "I'm living with Tom again. Lucky for me his new roommate moved out at the right time." He sighed heavily. "Anyway, he welcomed me back."

She gave him the sad look, the one he'd learned to loathe. "How're you doing with everything?"

He nodded. "I'm okay."

She put her hand to her forehead. "I'm sorry. I

didn't mean to give you that look."

He played dumb. "What look?"

"That cringe-worthy *I feel sorry for you* look."

"I'm used to it."

"Yeah, but you shouldn't have to be. I know what that's like. I wanted nothing more than for people to just stop asking me how I was doing and I just did the same thing to you. I'm sorry."

"It's okay, Ashley. Don't sweat it."

She then twisted her sweetly curved lips to one side. "What're you doing for lunch? Let me take you out so we can catch up."

He frowned reflexively. It had been so long since someone other than Tom just asked him such a basic question he didn't even know how to answer it.

She tilted her head and leaned in. "Is that a yes or a no?"

Shaking it off, he replied, "Yeah, okay." But he didn't mean to say yes.

They headed toward the shop door. As he nodded to the crusty shopkeeper behind the counter, Jake caught a glimpse of a grainy picture. He stopped to get a closer look. He was shocked. "What is that?"

The shopkeeper curled a partial smile. "You like it?" he said with a wink. "Took it myself."

"What? When? Where?"

"Down near Fort Fisher, about twenty years ago." The keeper leaned in close to Jake and let out a direct whisper, "You've seen something, haven't you?"

Jake met the old man's cloudy gray eyes and

then glanced over at Ashley. "I don't know what you're talking about."

The man's crooked smile straightened as he leaned back into the wall. "Of course you don't."

Jake quickly got himself together and headed outside. The air refused to stay in his lungs. He felt queasy.

"Hey, you okay?" Ashley reached out as he sped by her.

He nodded. "I'm fine."

"You don't look fine."

"It's just…" He trailed off and blew a long breath as his hands went to his waist. "Maybe we can do dinner another time."

Ashley narrowed her big brown eyes and pursed her lips. "No."

He snapped his head back. "No?"

"No."

"No what?"

"No, we're going right now. You're not backing out because you saw some random fake picture of a mermaid that reminded you of Cassie."

Jake studied her face. "It didn't remind me of…how do you know it's fake?"

"C'mon, Jake, you know how these roadside places are. They just try to sucker the tourists into paying big bucks for anything. That old clown was just playing up on you."

"But I'm not a tourist."

"He doesn't know that."

Jake chewed his lips.

"Look, Jake. I'm not going to let you wallow in self-pity any more. It's been over a year, well over a year. You have to start moving on. You have to get over it. I know what you're going through."

He snapped. "No, you don't. You didn't kill your parents." He regretted his words instantly. "I'm sorry."

She crossed her arms. "I was twelve. Can you imagine how hard it is to lose your entire family at twelve years old? You're right, no one is ever going to know exactly what you're going through, we all grieve differently. But I know what you're going through as much as anyone. I know what it's like to lose people you love too soon."

He took a few quick steps toward the sandy trail leading to the beach and fought the tears. "I just can't let go. I feel the pain every minute, every day. I close my eyes and I hear her screams and the gurgles of air as the life escaped her body. She knew I killed her and she hated me for it."

"My God, Jake, would you listen to yourself? You sound like an idiot."

He glanced at her but said nothing, because he had nothing to say.

She continued, "You don't know what the hell you're talking about. You're torturing yourself because you feel guilty."

"I deserve to feel guilty. It's my fault."

She raised her voice. "For God's sake, it was an accident. It was a horrible damned accident. It wasn't premeditated. They're gone, you can't bring them back. You can't bring *her* back."

"Don't you think I know that?" he yelled.

"I'm not sure you do." She snapped back and got in his face. "You need to stop this." She grabbed his arm, hard. "I ran into you today for a reason. You need to stop!"

He bit his lip so hard it nearly drew blood. "You don't know what I've gone through. You can't just show up in my life and—"

"Just show up?" She cut him off forcefully. "Are you kidding me? Jake, I tried to contact you a hundred times. I texted you. I called you. I drove to your house. You never once picked up the phone, you never once acknowledged me. A simple *I'm okay* would've been fine."

She stepped whisper-close to him. "I know you're hurting still. But Jake, you have to let her go. I'm here for you. I can help." She released his arm. "You don't have to suffer forever. You're a good man. Don't let one moment of tragedy ruin your life. You lived, they didn't. If you let yourself die too, that moment will have taken three lives. Do you understand that?"

He wiped his tears away with the back of his hand. "I just feel like I can't get out of this hole. I've wanted to die because it's easier than living. I have nothing left to live for."

"We all have something to live for. Sometimes it feels like we don't, but we do. After my parents and sister died, I was numb for months. Then after the numbness went away, I fell into depression, where it felt like I wanted to die every day. If I'd been old enough to have had the courage to kill myself, we might not be having this conversation. I still get depressed over it. I wondered how God could be so cruel to take them all from my life, to take so many people from the world in one day, in one moment. I wondered how different my life could have been. My sister would have been graduating college this year. I imagine where she would've gone and how proud my mom would've been. It's sad, really. You never get over it. But what you do get, Jake, is stronger, and smarter, and more perceptive into other people's pain. You can't let that one moment ruin you. You are meant to be here. Just like I am. I wasn't on that trip and in that building. We were both spared for a reason."

He looked up to the blue sky. "I'm just not sure *how* to move on." He reached up to his chest and held a fist over his heart. "I feel like it's broken beyond repair and I can't get over her."

She touched his balled fist. "I'll help you. We're friends, Jake. Nothing can take that away. I care about you. I value our friendship probably more than you know. It hurt me when you cut me out, when you wouldn't let me help you."

"I didn't want anyone to help me."

"I know, but I still wanted to. You mean a lot to me, you always have. You wouldn't let me help you then, but let me help you now. Please, I won't take no for an answer. Not this time, not ever again." She smiled. "Like I said, I ran into you for a reason. The universe wanted us to find each other today for some reason."

He cracked a slight smile. "The universe, huh?" It was a joke they'd shared before.

"You heard me."

"It's a small world."

"Not that small."

He nodded and let a drawn-out sigh escape. He

24

knew Ashley well enough to know that he couldn't win an argument against her. Not when she knew she was right. "Okay."

"Okay. Now let's go get some food."

Chapter 5

Jake felt a lot better after spending time with Ashley. He hadn't laughed like that in a long time. She'd always been able to crack him up with the simplest turn of phrase. It was the first time he'd gone a solid hour without thinking about Cassie since he could recall.

They didn't talk about anything of consequence. They just talked about the news, sports, the simple days when they were friends, and the fun times they had over a glass of wine, or a beach Frisbee game.

Ashley was a good friend...no, she was a great friend, even if a little part of him hated her for what she'd done to him a few years ago. He couldn't kid himself, his feelings for Ashley never quite went away. It was another reason he felt a little guilty over Cassie's death.

As the sun set into the horizon behind him, he settled on the same rock he'd been on last night and waited. He half expected Ariel wouldn't show up. The fact she may not really exist at all still sat heavy on his mind. His thoughts had been so

26

sketchy he wasn't sure he'd just spent two hours with Ashley, the girl who'd nearly wrecked his life before he wrecked it.

A couple of years ago, he would have never gone anywhere with Ashley. She was the hardest thing he ever had to get over in his life until Cassie's death. Seeing her face used to mess him up for a week. But now seeing her was different. It was a completely different feeling. It was easy to be with Ashley, and completely forget the loss of Cassie. Not because he didn't love Cassie, but because it sort of brought him back to a time before the loss. Life was great back then.

A few straggling fishermen packed up their things and headed off the beach, done for the evening. A quick glance around confirmed he was the last remaining person. The townhouses on the water to his left provided a soft glow, and to his right there was nothing but darkness on the small cove beach. Somewhere behind him, the walls of Fort Fisher told their stories of history to the wind and the slanting oaks that leaned away from the ocean, wincing away from her cooling mist, sang the songs of a hundred years.

The longer he sat the stupider he felt. He wasn't even sure why he was here, all he was doing was feeding his delusions of grandeur that were obviously some sort of coping mechanism. His mother would definitely say he was projecting his pain into a delusion. Sometimes growing up with a psychotherapist for a mother was terrible for the psyche. He was constantly unbending the roads of his mind she'd managed to twist.

After what felt like a long time, Jake was all but certain she wasn't showing up. Maybe the time with Ashley grounded him back to reality and his mind was clearing. It was amazing what a couple of hours with a friend could do.

Just a few seconds from leaving, she appeared in the waves a hundred feet out with a waving arm. An odd struggle of excitement and disappointment filled up his body as he stood. He shouldn't feel so good about cracking up, but in a way it was somewhat freeing. Maybe if his mind broke the rest of the way, he wouldn't have to worry about any hesitation in killing himself. He could easily jump in front of a speeding train.

Jake moved down the rocks toward the water, getting as close as he could. He was teetering on the edge, eyeing the thick wooden posts below. A jump onto them might prove risky and he could end up in the water if they were too slick. But he said to hell with it and jumped.

He hit the beam, his one foot slipped, and he ended up doing a split and falling into the water. Spinning quickly, he got his hands back onto the pylon and pulled himself up to a sitting position. There was no point in worrying about getting wet now.

Ariel jumped up and spit water out of her mouth like a fountain. "That was a funny moment."

Jake pushed his black hair back. "Not for me."

"Why'd you attempt such a move?"

He wiped his face. "I wanted to get closer to see you."

"And what do you see?"

28

He shook his head slowly. "Stunning beauty."

She leaned her elbows on the post between his legs. "I bet you say that to all the girls."

"Not all of them."

"Are you coming here for me now?"

He showed his open hands. "I don't have a gun."

She batted her big blue eyes. "So you've moved on to better things."

"I guess."

"Why did you want to die?"

He sighed. "It's a long story."

"Time is all we have. Nothing else in life belongs to us but the time we have here on this earth."

Jake looked at her. "How old are you? Did I ask you that already?"

"Age is only the number of years we wish to count. It is not a true indication of our self or our time spent. Age is relative. Time is not how many moments you've lived, it's how you've lived the moments you've had."

He laughed. "You talk like a riddle."

"Life is a riddle. Life is a puzzle, with pieces cut into shapes and strewn about all over your travels. Piece by piece we collect the sections and try to build the picture."

"Who *are* you?"

"I am Ariel. Who are you?"

"Jake."

"Jake, like Jake Davis?"

"Jake Wheeler."

"Jake Davis was a writer."

He shrugged. "Never heard of him."

"Do you read books?"

"Not really. Do you?"

"I've read thousands of books. Sometimes I read ten books a month."

"Whoa, I don't think I've read ten books in my whole life."

"I love to read. There are so many fantastical adventures between the pages of books. I live them."

"I like to watch movies."

"On television?"

"Of course, where do you watch movies?"

"I don't have a television."

"Where do you live?"

"On a little island up the river."

"Which island?"

She coyly looked away. "It doesn't have a name. And it's not a real island, it's just got water around it."

"Where is it?"

"Somewhere."

"You won't tell me?"

"I can't tell anyone. It's against the rules."

"Whose rules?"

"Father makes the rules."

"Is your father a mermaid too? Or a merman, whatever."

"You ask many questions."

"Well forgive me. I'm still trying to come to grips and believe I'm talking to a mermaid. It's still freaking me out that you're here."

"It shouldn't. I'm not freaking out about talking to you."

"Why me?"

"What do you mean?"

"I mean, you don't talk to everyone, do you?"

"No, I don't. I don't talk to anyone."

"So why did you choose me?"

"You chose me."

"Huh? I don't understand."

She turned her eyes away from him to the sky. "You were filled with such profound sadness. More sadness than I'd ever seen anyone filled with that I felt it in my heart. I started watching you each night. I felt like you needed a friend more than anyone I'd ever seen."

Jake looked up to the nearly full moon and wondered how his mind could craft such a richly detailed hallucination. But maybe this was what he needed to get over the pain. Maybe this was his mind's way of keeping him off that edge of suicide.

"Why are you so sad?"

Jake tried not to cry, but the tears welled up in his eyes with an ease he'd gotten too used to. "I lost someone close to me."

"I'm sorry. That must be hard."

"But the worst part is that it's my fault." His tears burst forth in a frantic fit. He lowered his head to his knees and let go. He felt like the despair was going to claim his life until Ariel touched his knee, squeezed it softly, and in a moment, she was real.

"You should talk about it. It will be easier," she said.

He met her eyes. They were so incredibly blue they didn't even look real. Even in the moonlight, he could see their amazing stark sharpness. They were so enchanting he started telling the story without even thinking. "I was driving. My fiancée Cassie and my best friend Paul were with me. We were coming back from the dress rehearsal for our wedding. Cassie wanted a big wedding, I didn't. But I wanted to give her what she wanted because I loved her. Cassie had a way of getting what she wanted. Not just from me, from anyone." He smiled. "She was one of those people you just knew had everyone wrapped around her finger but you loved her for it because she never abused that power. She was never demanding, never presumptuous."

"You loved her a great deal."

He wiped away a few tears. "I did, more than anything. She was an easy person to love, she made it easy to want to be with her." He shook his head slowly. "But I did a stupid thing."

"Talk about it."

He looked away, then back at her. It had to be another illusion, but her eyes seemed to get so big they were going to swallow him up. "It was just a regular night. The stars were out, the roads were dry, and there wasn't even a lot of traffic since most of the tourists weren't in town yet. It was just before Easter weekend." He started crying again. "But these jerks from Delaware in this white Mercedes, I remember focusing on their stupid license plate that said ***RICHBOY***, it just pissed me off so much. They cut us off and started messing with us, swerving and slamming on the brakes and being aggressive. Then one of them threw a beer bottle out of the car. It smashed off the hood of my car and cracked my windshield. I had this really nice car, a Nissan 350z...it was a beauty, fire engine red, with black wheels."

He looked up. After a momentary pause, he continued. "They were just taunting us and I got mad. I got so mad I started chasing them. I don't even know why. It was just like something that came over me. Cassie was yelling at me, asking me to stop. But I kept chasing them with this tunnel vision. I couldn't see anything but the back of their car. No matter how fast they went, I just kept chasing. I never even saw the stop sign. I never saw the cross street. The next thing I know I see the lights of a pickup truck coming right at us, right at Cassie's side of the car." The tears overwhelmed him, he could hardly talk, but he kept going. "I tried to turn, or stop, or speed up—anything to avoid it, but there was no time."

Jake broke down. He couldn't speak anymore. He slumped into himself and felt like he was going to melt into the waves. If Ariel had not been there to hold him up, he would have slid into the ocean and drowned. But she was there. And for the first time he knew without question, she was real. It was that thought that quickly pulled him together. This was impossible, yet it was right here.

He leveraged himself back upright.

"That's a sad story. But it doesn't sound like your fault."

He shook his head. "The driver of the truck was drunk, more than twice the legal limit. But I ran the stop sign, I was speeding. But I could have let it go. I had numerous chances to let it go, to turn away, to be the bigger man. But I didn't. I let a stupid mistake ruin so many lives. I had a choice." He punched his chest with each word. "I had a choice."

Ariel touched his arm. "Life is a series of choices, of roads we choose. Each one leads us to yet another road filled with choices. Sometimes we choose wrongly, but sometimes those wrong choices lead to something worthy."

"I don't see anything worthy in needless death. I'm a killer. I may not have premeditated it, but I'm a killer."

"No, you're not a killer."

"I feel like one."

"Killers are bad people. You are not a bad person, Jake. I can tell you have a wonderful soul and a kind heart. We must not let our mistakes of the past define our futures. We all make mistakes. It is what being alive is all about."

"You know how to put things."

"I have had a lot of time to think about the world. I wish sometimes I didn't think so much." Ariel glanced up to the sky. "It is almost time for me to go. It's getting too dark."

He nodded. "You held me up."

"What do you mean?"

"I was about to fall into the water. You kept me from falling."

"Of course. Why wouldn't I?"

He searched the sky. "That means you're real."

She chuckled. "Of course I'm real. I've been trying to tell you."

"But it's impossible. You're amazing."

She pushed away from the shore, swimming on

her back a few strokes. "Nothing is impossible, Jake. If you believe enough, the world's impossibilities become realities."

With that, she disappeared under the surface and didn't return.

Chapter 6

Ashley

Ashley rolled out of bed. The moment her feet touched the cold wood floor she felt like she wanted to curl up and slip back under the covers. Her head was not clear yet after drinking damn near the entire bottle of wine.

She heard Mike downstairs clanking around in the kitchen already. It was just unnatural for anyone to be that energetic on a Saturday morning.

Stretching her pink t-shirt down to cover up a little, she ambled down the steps and out to the kitchen.

"Good morning for me, but I bet not for you," Mike said sarcastically as he poured coffee into a black mug.

"Ugh, I feel like crap."

"Well, you shouldn't have consumed so much alcohol."

"Thanks, Captain Obvious." She poured coffee into her favorite mug with the dolphin on the side.

"I told you. You never listen to me anymore, just do whatever the heck you want with willful disregard for your health."

After her first luxurious sip, she replied, "I don't need a classic Mike Robertson lecture right now. I'm not a child."

"Then don't do stupid things and then complain about them. If you act like a teenager, I'm going to lecture you as the only adult in this house."

She gave him a dirty look, and he gave it right back. The fact that Mike was a morning person and she wasn't was really only one of the problems in her marriage. And it was a small problem at that. But starting your day off with a stressful conversation wasn't really conducive to kicking things off with a smile.

Her mother once said, "A *woman needs to be with a man that can make her smile first thing in the morning.*" That sounded simple enough, but you'd be surprised. If a boy can make you laugh even when you're cranky, or tired, or even angry, then he is true keeper.

Mike wasn't much for making her laugh. He was handsome, made good money, and he loved her. But sometimes he was just too good, too uptight, too annoyingly proper. Sometimes she just wanted him to make an inappropriate joke and do something silly. Mike didn't do silly...ever. He didn't do playful or goofy. He didn't do a lot of things that didn't seem important at the time she married him. He was an adult, and it was lame.

By the time she got to the bottom of her coffee mug she felt like another cup would be a waste. Her head was clear and she wanted some food.

"So what's on your agenda today?" Mike asked as he bit into an apple with a crunch. "I hope it involves putting some clothes on."

She ignored the latter comment. "I'm not sure. What about you?"

"I told you last night. I'm meeting Brett and Hal for golf. Why do you think I'm dressed like this?"

She looked at him and rolled her eyes. "I guess…whatever."

"I swear, Ash, sometimes I wonder if you listen to anything I say."

"Excuse me for forgetting some insignificant detail you told me after I was done drinking a bottle of wine."

"Which is why I told you to stop after the second glass. If you're going to act like a teenager—"

"Please, Mike." She slammed her mug down harder than she meant. "Not right now. I don't want to hear it."

"Well, you're going to hear it because I—"

"Seriously, not now. Shut up! I can't even listen to your mouth. It makes me want to punch you."

"Well, that's mature. Threats of physical violence, is that what we've come to? Really mature. Really—really mature."

"Who gives a flying shit about mature?"

"Nice mouth, real lady-like of you."

"Nice shirt, did your mom pick that out?"

He looked at her and shook his head. "I swear, Ashley, you're never going to change."

"Thank God for that."

He stared at her for a long bit. The marriage

counselor suggested that when this happened that they try to talk it out. She wanted a divorce but Mike did not. He wanted to try counseling first, but after six months, nothing was better. They hadn't had sex in about seven months, and she didn't even miss it. It was never that good, anyway.

After neither one of them said anything for several minutes, Ashley finally said, "Maybe we need to reconsider things. The sessions are obviously not working."

He rolled his eyes. "Whatever. I'm leaving. Have fun dealing with your hangover."

"Have fun playing with your little white balls." She curled a smile. She'd wanted to say that to him every time he went golfing, but didn't want to start him off on something. But since they were already annoyed at each other, it didn't matter and she needed a laugh.

"Oh, that's very funny. You're a real comedienne, you should go on tour." He stormed out of the kitchen through the door that led to the garage.

She went over to the cabinet and took out a box of cereal for breakfast, but then decided to put it back as Mike sped away in his white convertible BMW. Instead, she grabbed her keys and headed outside to her car. It took her about halfway across the lawn and a wide-eyed grin and wave from the fifty-something man across the street, for her to realize she wasn't wearing any pants.

After spinning around quickly, she went back inside to get dressed, choosing some black yoga pants and a blue V-neck t-shirt.

In her car, she sat for a few moments. She'd thought about doing this all night, but now that the time had come, she was somewhat hesitant and she didn't even know why. It didn't matter, she was going.

* * *

Jake

Jake woke up when the knocking on the door got louder and more urgent. It became less of a knock and more of a pounding. He rolled off the bed and staggered to the hallway.

A quick glance over at Tom's room revealed both he and his long board were gone. He was no doubt privy to some early morning waves and took off before sunrise.

Shuffling over the red and orange carpet that lined the hall, he got to the front door and saw Ashley standing behind the glass. He pulled open the door.

"Hey," she said.

"Ashley, what's up?"

She pushed her way into the house. "I decided I'm no longer going to allow you to wallow in your sorrow. So get dressed, we're going to get some breakfast." She looked him up and down. "Did you sleep in your clothes?" Then she sniffed him. "Did you sleep in your wet clothes?"

Jake pulled at his shirt. "Uh, yeah, sorta."

"Why were you swimming in cargo shorts?"

"I...well, I wasn't swimming as much as I was

falling in."

She turned her head and looked at him with the side of her eye. "Ooh—kay." She walked to the fridge. "Well, take a shower and get dressed. You're taking me out to Poppies for a giant veggie omelet and pancakes."

"I am?"

"Yes, you are."

Jake looked at her for a few seconds. She widened her big brown eyes even more, and without saying a word, urged him to get going. He did.

After a quick shower and a typical shorts and t-shirt outfit, they headed out to Ashley's silver Mazda sedan.

Jake wiped his eyes. "What happened to your Jeep?"

"Mike made me sell it."

"Why?"

"He said it wasn't safe. But really it was his stupid parents. They said only lesbians drive Jeeps and it bothered him so much he just would not shut up about it. I sold it to shut him up."

"Oh, wow."

"Yeah, they're assholes." As she approached the car, she tossed him the keys. "Here, you drive."

Jake caught the keys and froze. He looked down at them. He'd driven plenty since the accident but he hadn't driven with anyone else in the car.

Ashley walked around to the passenger side and stood by the door. "You know how to do it. Now get in the car and drive."

He looked up at her. Again, she urged him with her eyes, and again he complied and got into the car. The anxiety he thought he'd have sort of just drained away as he backed out of the driveway and eased down the one-lane street.

"I knew you could do it," she said with a large hint of sarcasm.

"You're the first person I've driven with."

"It'll be fine."

The short drive to Poppies didn't stress him at all. It was all very normal. They pulled up to the wooden building with the large yellow and blue sign that read *'Poppies Diner'* and parked. It always bothered Jake that the name of this place seemed to be grammatically incorrect. Although perhaps it wasn't. Maybe there were more than one Poppy. Perhaps it was named after the flower, or the poppy seed.

The place was nice enough inside, and the food was definitely good. They ended up being seated in the farthest booth in the back, which was fine by Jake. He preferred to be in the back.

A perky little blonde waitress took their orders and scampered away. She reminded Jake of Ariel and his face must have said something because Ashley asked, "Do you know her?"

He quickly shook it off. "No, she just reminded me of someone maybe."

"Cassie? She does kind of look like Cassie."

Jake shot a look at Ashley and considered her thought. The concept made him think all over again that maybe Ariel was indeed a creation of his mind and nothing more. The fact that she did resemble Cassie kind of spooked him. He hadn't really considered it but it made some sense.

"Are you okay?" Ashley asked.

"I'm...I don't know."

"Have you seen anyone, Jake? I mean professionally speaking."

"Yeah, I saw two different doctors."

"Not your mother's colleagues, I hope."

"No, definitely not."

"Did you feel like it helped you at all?"

He shrugged. "I don't know, not really. It was all the standard stuff."

She nodded. "After my parents died, I saw about five different specialists. None of it really helped."

"What did?"

"Time, just time. And good friends to help make new memories. Surrounding myself with positive people helped a lot." She sipped the glass of orange juice the waitress set down as she spun away. "We had a family friend and she basically picked me up by my shirt and said 'You need to live. You need to live for you, and you need to live for them.'"

Jake sipped his juice. "It sounds so easy."

"It is easy. You just have to make a choice to do it. A terrible thing happened to you, Jake. And yes, actions you took directly contributed to that outcome. But it wasn't malicious. You didn't mean for anything bad to happen. You didn't let those punks provoke you out of some desire to hurt anyone in that car. You didn't chase them thinking an accident was going to happen. That's why they're accidents."

"I know. I've told myself that a hundred times but I just keep going back. At one point, Cassie yelled at me. She said, '*It's not worth it, let it go.*'

But by the time I heard those words and understood what they really meant, I was already in the intersection. It was too late."

"Sometimes we make mistakes. That's what makes us human. But we don't have to pay for those mistakes forever. At least we shouldn't. We don't have to punish ourselves for impetuous choices for life, and we don't have to die to be forgiven."

He met her eyes. Her words were as if someone hit him with a tree branch. They shook him to the bone. An undeniable theme was storming into his life, and both Ariel and Ashley were delivering the same message at the same time. It was weird, and oddly serendipitous. He sucked a deep breath and centered himself just as the waitress dropped their food on the table.

As the server turned away, Ashley reached across the table and grabbed his hand. "Jake, think about it. Would Cassie want you to hate yourself? Was she that kind of person?"

He shook his head. "No, she wasn't."

"Exactly. She'd never in a million years want to see you like this. You know what she'd say? She'd say..." She trailed off and motioned with hinting hands.

Jake thought about it for a moment then Cassie's words came to him. "She'd say there's too much magic in the world to be sad."

"Exactly. Cassie was pure joy. She was probably the happiest person I've ever known. She believed in joy, magic, and all kinds of wonder. She understood more than most people that life is a gift

44

and every day that gift can bring us joy. But your joy did not die with her, Jake. You had joy long before her and you'll have it long after. It's okay to be happy again. It's what she's screaming at you from the beyond right now. She's telling you to be happy, you just have to listen to your heart. Her words are in there and will be forever."

He knew she was right, and as her hand slid back across the table to the fork that leaned on the plate, Jake felt something he had not felt in months. He felt relieved, and he felt like he wanted to spend time with someone other than himself. He felt like maybe he had just turned a corner, and this time he didn't even crash.

Chapter 7

Castro

He went only by the name Castro, though that wasn't even his real name. It's just what he told his clients. Sometimes he wasn't even sure of his real name anymore since he never used it and had not spoke it in probably twenty years. He had no real driver's license, no real credit cards, and no bank accounts. He worked only with cash and stayed only in hotels and short-term rentals that didn't require credit checks. It was the life he'd chosen, it was the life he loved. He never had to make friends, he paid for sex when he wanted it, he spent every holiday alone, and that was just fine with him.

He lived a life of total autonomy. He worked when he wanted and picked only the jobs that paid the best money. He made a ton of cash, and he saved almost all of it because he knew how to live cheaply. His plan was to retire in a couple years and disappear into the landscape, probably in the Bahamas.

Watching his latest job through the binoculars, he jotted down some notes onto the yellow pad. Unlike most people these days, Castro hated computers and tablets for taking notes. He preferred to write things on actual paper with an actual pen. It wasn't that he was too old to adapt, he just preferred the feeling and control of paper. Burning any piece of evidence with the tip of his cigarette was simple and effective.

He watched the subject, and the girl with whom he walked. She was not a target and didn't matter in this mission. If he had to kill the man however, and she was around, he would have to kill the girl too. No one had ever seen him at the scene of a job and lived. That's just the way it went. The fact he was good at cleaning up his loose ends was what allowed him to have such a long, lucrative career.

He dialed the number and put the phone to his ear. "This is Castro. I've got the subject in sight. What are your current wishes?"

The man on the other end cleared his throat. "Just keep an eye on him for now. I don't know that we have to do anything yet. Stay on him, take notes, and I will keep you updated."

"Understood."

"Watch his movements and be prepared to make a move when I say."

"Understood." He liked to let his clients think they had some measure of control over him, but they really didn't. He knew how to play the game and he played along when he had to for the sake of the job.

Castro ended the call and watched the subject

walk down the beach access. He lit a fresh cigarette and took a long drag. He loved to smoke. The feeling of the noxious fumes filling his lungs was just the best feeling in the world. He'd rather smoke than eat, and sometimes he did.

* * *

Jake

Jake kicked off his sandals and let his toes dig into the warm sand. It had been a long time since he just sat on the sand and didn't want to cry. Ashley had really taken his mind off the bad things. "Thank you, Ashley."

"For what?" She sat next to him on the edge of the dune and faced the ocean.

"For this." He motioned his hand between them. "For being my friend."

"Thank you for letting me."

He picked up a fistful of sand, sifting the grains in his hand. "You made it easy."

"You didn't." She laughed. "But I wasn't taking no for an answer this time."

"What made you decide to not take no for an answer this time?"

She shrugged. "Dunno, call it a gut feeling. I just felt like this time was right. I felt like you were finally ready. When I ran into you at such a random place, I just felt like it meant something. I can sense when people need a friend."

He huffed. "You've always had that quality."

"You're not the first person to tell me that."

A short chuckle escaped him. "You've always made me laugh."

"And you me. Of course, a lot of this is not based on how you are now, but how you were. I miss the old Jake. He was funny and smart and could just own the room when he wanted to. He didn't always want to and that made him even more desirable to be around. The world deserves to get him back."

"I want to get him back. I know he's in there. And for the first time since the accident I feel like I can reach him." He met her eyes. "I feel like you reached him."

She patted him on the knee. "Only because you stopped being an ass."

He nodded, pausing for a beat before he asked, "How's your life? I mean, how's Mike and everything?"

She shrugged. "It is what it is. Mike is good looking, he's smart, he makes good money. He loves me."

"That sounded totally rehearsed."

She blew out a breath. "That's fair. I don't know, maybe it is."

"I always liked Mike."

She moved her head back and made a face. "Really?"

Jake laughed a bit. "No, not really. Quite honestly he's a douche bag and I always thought you deserved better."

"He never liked you either. All that time we used to spend together, he was jealous for sure—especially those late nights. Man, I used to hear it all the time. Wasn't Cassie jealous too?"

"Not really. She knew we were working and understood."

"Would she have understood if…" She looked out to the water. "You know."

Jake dusted the sand off his hands. "You mean the night of the aloe plant?"

She blew out a long breath. "Yeah, the aloe plant."

Jake tipped his head back. He'd never said what he was about to say, but at this point in life he didn't care about hiding truths. "I never wanted to kiss anyone more than I wanted to kiss you that night."

She let out an uncomfortable laugh. "I know. That was the only time I even came close to ruining my marriage vows."

"I almost ruined mine before I took them. I had just proposed to Cassie like the week before."

"I know. I felt so guilty because Cassie was my friend too."

"It scared me. I kept thinking that maybe I shouldn't even be getting married if I could fall in love with another woman so easily."

She looked at him as her mouth fell open. "You never told me you were in love with me."

Jake smiled. "Ashley, I was so in love with you it messed me up for months. Here I was planning a wedding to a woman I loved more than life itself, the whole time I was in love with someone else too. I didn't understand how someone could love two people, but I did."

She nodded softly. "I think it's totally possible to

love two people at once."

"It shouldn't be that easy. I mean, you're an awesome person. But it shouldn't have been that easy for me."

She shrugged. "Maybe it was easy for a reason. It was easy for me too, Jake. I could have easily thrown away my entire life for you. Did you feel that?"

"I asked myself a hundred times. What if I'd never met Cassie and you'd never met Mike? Where would we be? I wonder what would have happened if I had kissed you."

She looked away to the sea as some pelicans skimmed the surface in perfect formation. "Sometimes I think God likes to use me as a sounding board for jokes."

"I'm right there with you."

They let the topic fade for a moment, then Ashley asked, "Have you heard from your parents at all?"

Jake pursed his lips. "My mother called like a month ago. Her newest boyfriend has a boat, a big boat—a full time captain, crew, and chef kind of boat. She's in the Bahamas or Cuba, who knows. She's made it a habit to run away with her rich clients."

"Mind shrinker of the rich and famous."

"This is like the third one in five years. The last guy she married for like six months."

"How many times has she been married now?"

"Counting my father, like five."

"She's a train wreck." She threw a shell. "What about your dad?"

"Dad, well, let's see...he's in Europe again somewhere, totally out of money and living out of a backpack. I have no idea where he is exactly, as he refuses to carry a cellphone. He was in like Switzerland for a while, but I think he's in Germany now. I haven't spoken to him in six months. But last I heard he was shacked up with a girl like barely old enough to drink. Some Dutch girl."

"That's crazy. I would give anything to have just one parent, and you have two that are completely useless."

"I guess irony comes in all forms."

"You can say that again." Ashley laughed. "Do you remember when your Dad gave away his car, and your mother hit him with the frying pan?"

Jake laughed. "Ridiculous. I figured Cassie was going to back out of the relationship right then. I tried to tell her my parents were crazy, but I don't think she expected next level crazy. But she was totally cool with all of it."

"It must have been insane growing up with them."

"It was a circus. Opposites might attract, but they definitely should not stay together long enough to have a kid."

"I wish I would have known you then."

He smiled at her. "We would've had some fun."

Ashley stood up. "C'mon, there's a volleyball game down there. Let's go join it."

They headed down the beach about a quarter mile and asked to join in. The players were happy to add in another couple people and Jake was happy they allowed. It felt so good just to release some

52

energy and sweat in the sun.

Ordinarily he'd probably take off his shirt and get a tan, but he didn't have any sun block on. He'd always had a good physique and maintained it not at the gym, but generally doing beach sports like surfing, kayaking, and volleyball. He also spent a considerable amount of time on his mountain bike. He'd long been an avid mountain bike rider, but since the accident he'd not really done it. He'd stopped doing most of the things he'd loved.

This huffing and puffing in the hot summer sun was exactly what he needed. And although he was thinking about her, he didn't miss Cassie right now. It was the first time since the accident he actually felt like he was getting over it.

After the game, they headed back to the car, stopping off at one of the Carolina Beach boardwalk stands to grab a drink. It was getting close to dinnertime.

"Thanks, Ashley, for today. It was great. I really appreciate it."

"Well, I just appreciate you." She took a long sip of her sports drink. "Why don't you come for dinner? Mike might like to see you."

Jake laughed. "Mike won't ever like to see me…ever."

"No, you're probably right. But screw him, it's my house too and I can invite my friend for dinner."

"I appreciate it, but I think I'm just going to chill the rest of the day and get to sleep early." He was only partially telling the truth. As the sun drew closer to the horizon, he kept thinking of Ariel more with each hour.

"Are you okay? You seem to be preoccupied with something."

He gave her a look. He'd forgotten how intuitive Ashley was. He didn't know if she was like this with everyone, but the two of them always shared a very uncanny, unspoken link. She always seemed to know what he was thinking. "It's like you're in my brain."

She playfully hit his arm. "Oh my God, I haven't said that in so long."

He nodded. They used to say that to each other all the time because it was so true. "Me either."

"With that in mind, tell me what you're thinking."

He wanted to tell her, he really did. But he didn't want her to think he was crazy. The mermaid still wasn't real. And she would remain unreal until he said something about her out-loud. It was like tempting fate. If he admitted she was real to someone else, he might go full on crazy. Or it might make her disappear forever, and part of him didn't want that, either.

He looked at Ashley. "Let me ask you something."

"Shoot."

"After your parents and sister died, did you ever feel like you were going crazy?"

She nodded. "Of course, for a long time."

"Did you ever, you know, imagine things?"

Ashley nodded. "All the time. I'd think I heard my mother's voice. I'd swear I saw my dad pulling in the driveway, and once I was missing a CD and I swore my sister took it."

"No, I mean, did you ever, like, have an imaginary friend?"

She looked at him. "It's like you're in my brain."

"Really?"

"Her name was Nicole. She was a stuffed animal, this little bear. I would talk to her whenever I needed someone to talk to. It got to the point that I was talking to her even when she wasn't with me."

"Where did she go?"

"I guess I just let her go after a while. She'd served her purpose."

"Huh."

"Why, are you seeing an imaginary friend?" She smiled slyly.

He shook his head. "No, no, I'm just curious."

She gave him a narrow-eyed stare. It was like she was looking right through him. And given her ability to know what was going on in his brain, he'd all but accepted the fact she knew he was lying.

"Well," Ashley said. "You can tell me anything you want. You know that, right?"

He nodded. "Thanks, Ashley." He hugged her. "You're a great friend."

Chapter 8

After his day of what most people might call normalcy, he felt almost like sitting on the rocks waiting for his illusion to return was tempting fate. Maybe he didn't need the illusion tonight, or ever again. Maybe it was enough to just see Ashley two days in a row and remember that it was not only possible, but perfectly okay, to feel something other than loss and pain.

He'd forgotten how hard it was to get over Ashley. There was no way he wanted to go through that again. But being with her, he could see how easy it would be to fall in love with her all over again. The fact she was married was a complete non-starter. He was definitely not a home-wrecker. That was his father's deal. He's the one that broke up marriages like it was his job. Of course, to be fair, his mother did it on a regular basis too. That, however, was not going to be him at any cost.

As the sundown filled the sky at his back, he wondered if Ariel would come. A few people in his immediate area would surely keep her from appearing. It was a little disappointing that his imagination couldn't create a better name than Ariel. That was so very lame. Of all the names in the world, he could have come up with something better than that. But no, he had to pick the only mermaid movie he'd ever actually seen in the history of mermaid movies.

A few minutes after the last person left his area, he moved down the large rocks closer to the water, hoping it wouldn't take him much longer to get into the deep regions of his brain. Maybe he needed to see Ariel more tonight than ever before, to once and for all dismiss her as an illusion. Maybe that's why he came here again rather than just giving up on it all.

Ashley definitely had him second-guessing his sadness. He'd been wallowing in it, enjoying the pain in a way, for so long he forgot what it was like to just exist. He didn't want to be sad anymore, he wanted to move on. There was light at the end of the tunnel and he was running toward it full speed.

The sea was rough. The waves were slamming into the large rocks, sending a huge spray into the air ten feet over his head. He didn't think there was any way Ariel would be able to stay at the base of these rocks and not get crushed.

With that in mind, he got up and started to navigate down the shore a little, to where the landing was softer. He got to the end and decided to head over to the sand where a small inlet between the breakers and the beach had long ago carved its way into the shore.

Jake took a short step and jumped over the wall,

landing on the sand next to the little inlet. He looked around and didn't see anyone. He was alone.

Cupping his hands to his mouth he yelled, "Ariel!" He'd never called her before. She usually just showed up.

She didn't show up at first but then he saw some movement out in the waves. The glint of something catching the moonlight grabbed his attention. She was out there, bobbing in the waves but not coming closer.

He had a good idea what was keeping her from coming into shore. Something compelled him to dive into the next big wave and start swimming toward her. Ducking under the last curl, he came up for air right next to her. "Hey."

"I wasn't sure if you were going to swim out to me."

"I wasn't at first. But it looked like you weren't going to come in."

"The waves are too big. I can't go to the shore when they're like that. It's just too hard to handle."

"You'll get slammed around."

"I do like to breathe." She winked. "You're a good swimmer."

"I've been swimming in these waves since I was five years old."

"Me too."

He laughed. "Yeah, I bet."

"Were you born here?"

"Yeah, right here in Wilmington."

"Lived here all your life?"

"No, I went to college up in New York City, stayed up there for a few years, but I missed the

58

beaches and the warm air."

"So you love to swim."

"I do. It's probably nice to have that fin."

She flipped over and kicked a bunch of water at him, popping back up after her somersault. "Jealous? It makes it easier to zoom through the water. I can out-swim anyone."

"But I bet it's harder to walk," he joked.

"Ha-ha, very funny."

"Sorry, that was a low blow."

"You're smiling. I've never seen you smile so big."

He treaded water against a big wave. "I am."

"That's great. I'm happy for you. You have a nice smile."

"It's been a while since I've had a reason to smile."

"Am I your reason to smile?"

"One of them."

"Even better if you have more than one."

"I was in such a good mood I didn't think you'd come."

Ariel ducked under the water and popped back up on the other side of him. "What sense does that make?"

Jake started to get tired from treading water. "I don't know. I just figured you were a result of my sadness."

She frowned. "I don't know how to take that. Your mood doesn't dictate whether or not I would come to see you."

"A part of me still kinda figured that you were a stress-induced hallucination."

She moved closer to him. "You still don't believe I'm real?"

He nervously laughed. "I'm just going to play it out until one day you disappear."

"How can I convince you?"

"I don't know."

She moved closer. So close he could feel her brushing against the length of his body. "Touch me," she said.

Jake felt nervous but he reached out and wrapped his arm around her waist. The soft undulations of her fin kept both of them buoyant in the rolling waves.

She whispered in his ear. "Do I feel real?"

"Terribly real."

They were cheek to cheek, but he felt her lips drawing close to his until they were kissing. Jake felt himself lost in her, and the water, and the world. He'd never had that floating feeling of kissing someone while he was actually floating under the power of something like this. He was kissing a dream, a fable. Either way, it was simultaneously the most bizarre and amazing moment of his life. But it was so real, so very real. The kiss was both innocent and sensual. He wanted to kiss her forever but there was one thing in the back of his mind.

She finally pulled back. "Now do you believe?"

He took a deep breath. "How could anyone deny that?"

"I can understand your skepticism."

"Can you blame me?"

"This is why I don't show myself to people often. It's not good for anyone."

60

"How many people have seen you?"

"A few."

"What happened?"

"Nothing happened. I didn't let them see me again."

"How come you let me see you again?"

"I like you. I know my secret will be safe with you. I trust you."

"Thank you for trusting me."

A car pulled into the parking area near the beach. The lights cast out into the water and fell briefly on them. Ariel quickly ducked under the waves. Jake sank with her. When the headlights extinguished, they popped back up.

She gave him another long kiss, and then kissed his neck softly. "I have to go." Letting him go so he could tread water again on his own, she said, "Until next time."

With that, she was gone again.

Jake treaded water for a few seconds and then headed back toward the shore. He got to the sand and removed his shirt, wringing it out and cursing himself for not taking it off before jumping in. He found his sandals in the sand where he'd left them and slid his feet into them.

As he approached the parking area, the driver of the car stood there smoking a cigarette. Jake walked up the beach to the gravel path and headed toward his car.

"Nice night for a swim," the man said.

Jake nodded. "Yeah, not bad."

"Gotta watch out for the sharks. They like to feed at night."

Jake kept walking. "I'm not too scared."

The man tipped his hat. "They like rare flesh. Be careful who you swim with, certain types of creatures attract them more than others."

Jake stopped. "What?"

"You gotta be careful when you're in the water. You can get in over your head really fast and before you know it, it's too late."

"Huh?"

"You spend too long in there and you'll never make it back to shore in time before you find yourself gasping for air that never comes."

Jake didn't reply this time. He just kept walking to his car as the man gave him a creepy cigarette-drag grin.

Chapter 9

Ashley

Ashley got out of the car at the same time Mike was exiting their three-car garage with a golf bag in his hand. He dropped it into the trunk of his car and closed the lid.

He stopped and put his hands on his narrow hips. "Where were you?"

"Out."

"Where?"

"With a friend."

"I saw Donna and Kelly at the gas station. They're your only friends."

She walked up the sidewalk. "I was with Jake."

"All day? Again?"

"Yeah, again. So what?"

He stepped in front of her. "I don't think it's good for you to be spending so much time with him."

She pushed past him. "I'll spend time with whoever I want." Opening the front door, she gave him one more look.

Mike entered the door before it closed. "What kind of attitude is that?"

She tossed her small pink purse on the counter. "It's the kind of attitude I've always had. Do you have a problem with it suddenly?"

"Jake is a loser."

She snapped him a dirty look. "You don't know him well enough to make that assessment. Jake is a nice guy having a hard time. He could use a friend."

"I know him enough. He's a shiftless loser from a loser family. And he drags down everyone he touches. You've seen him twice in two days. How much friend does he need?"

She went to the fridge and took out a plastic container full of baby carrots. "I don't know. How does one go about answering that asinine question?"

He shook his head. "You know what I mean. Why're you spending so much time with him? Does he even have a job anymore? I'm pretty sure his business is bankrupt by now."

"What does that matter?"

"I mean he's a loser. He's a beach bum."

"He's my friend, Mike. He's been my friend for a long time."

"He's a lost cause. The guy is a piece of garbage. Let him sink into the abyss and fall off the face of the Earth."

She was growing angrier by the moment. "Jake is not what you think."

"I know enough. I know people who worked with him. The guy had a great career and threw it all away to fix bicycles. What kind of loser does that?"

She sneered, "He bought a bike shop."

"He's a moron. He could have been on Wall Street. The guy gets handed a position at one of the most regarded investment firms on the planet and he quits to sell bikes to a bunch of drunks on the beach."

"You're crazy. He hated that work. Not everyone needs to make a lot of money to define themselves."

"He dragged Cassie down. She came from a good family. She was slumming around with him and look where that got her."

Ashley looked at him with complete contempt. "That's not fair. That's a shitty thing to say."

"He deserves to wallow in pain for what he did."

She felt the heat of anger welling up in her. She took a fistful of carrots and nearly whipped it at his head but she didn't want to waste the food. "You're a real jerk-off sometimes. That's really shitty. What the hell kind of attitude is that?"

He picked up his phone. "It's the same attitude I've always had."

"So you've always been a jerk-off?"

Pointing with his phone, he said, "Stay away from him. I don't want that loser dragging you down."

"Mike, what is this crap? Are you jealous of him?"

He moved closer to her. "Should I be? I mean, you tell me. Is there something going on with you two?"

"No, there isn't. We're good friends."

"Yeah, maybe he's playing you to get into your pants."

She huffed. "You're disgusting. You think he'd play on my sympathies to get a piece of ass?"

"I know men, it's what they do."

"Speak for yourself. Jake isn't like that. He never was and he certainly isn't going to start now." She resisted mentioning the fact that he'd cheated on her already. She knew it, but he didn't know that she knew. It was something she was keeping in her back pocket.

"Says you."

"Yeah, *says me*. And since you're supposed to love me, you'll trust me."

"Maybe I can trust you today but maybe not tomorrow. People break the bond of trust all the time. Tomorrow is another story. Maybe I've trusted you for the last time. Maybe I'm done trusting you tomorrow. I have a career here, and a public image."

"Fuck you!" She let that slip. It just came out, she didn't usually swear at him. "Is that what this is about? Your career? Your public reputation? You think you're going to sell fewer houses if there's a Robertson family scandal? You're a complete slimeball."

"I'm done with you and your childish behavior. Done! I can't live like this. I'm tired of being the only adult in this relationship." He stormed out the door and slammed it hard behind him.

Ashley took a deep breath and popped a carrot into her mouth. She chewed so hard and fast she bit the inside of her lip and drew blood. With a shake of her head, she tossed the rest of the carrots into the container and probed the cut on her bottom lip with her tongue.

Mike had a knack lately for getting under her skin. But they were just weeks away from their eighth anniversary and she honestly didn't know if she was going to make it another day.

Her old boss Lynn had warned her not to marry Mike about a hundred times. The entire time they were engaged, Lynn was ending her marriage of fifteen years. She was so anti-marriage that Ashley didn't take anything she said seriously. Looking back now, so much of what she'd said was making sense.

The biggest thing that kept sticking out was that a few months ago she had a suspicion that Mike was having an affair. When she found out the truth, she didn't even care. The fact she didn't care was what seemed too stark in relation to everything. If she really loved him, that idea would crush her. Instead, all it did was make her wonder why she didn't care.

If he had not cheated, it didn't even matter. She knew in her heart that she didn't love him anymore the way she once did. But maybe that was normal. Things change, people change, and feelings change. Yet marriages march on for decades undaunted, laughing in the face of the incredibly high divorce rate. Hers, however, was not meant to be one of them.

* * *

Castro

Castro waited on the pier. The darkness

swallowed him up, just the way he liked. His phone rang and he answered without a word.

The voice on the other end was clean and emotionless. "Your last report was troublesome."

"I just report what I see."

"I think we should act now before it gets out of hand."

"That's your call."

"I think it's for the best."

"How should I proceed?"

There was a long silence on the other side of the phone. "I think I'll leave that up to you. But give me some time to do background. I want to know exactly who he is before we proceed."

"Very well."

"I have to make sure he's not tied back to the organization in any respect."

"I assure you he's not. He's a mixed up kid, that's it."

"All due respect, I like to know who I'm having—"

"Careful what you say."

"Don't worry, I'm discreet. And I pay well. So give me a couple days."

"That's your call."

"In the meantime, just try to scare him away and see how he responds. Maybe we don't have to proceed if he runs for the hills."

"And if he doesn't scare?"

"Why wouldn't he scare?"

"Not everyone runs away at the prospect of a fight. Some people dig in their heels and push back."

"Then we will have no choice but to proceed with extreme measures."

"Very well." He ended the call and lit a cigarette.

Chapter 10

Jake

Jake thought he was dreaming when the strange noises invaded his ears. But even after blinking himself awake, the sound still existed.

He sat up in bed, listening. It sounded as if someone was throwing something at the house, or it was raining rocks. But it wasn't raining.

After swinging his feet to the floor, he walked down the hallway, stopping in front of Tom's open bedroom door. "Tom, you awake?" A soft snoring noise answered his question. That guy could sleep through a plane crashing into the house.

Continuing down the hallway, Jake thought the clunking noise had stopped. After a few seconds of silence, it appeared that was indeed the case. He pressed forward to the kitchen, to the side door where the noise seemed to have been most prevalent.

He looked outside into the early morning light but didn't see anything. Cracking open the door, he stepped out onto the concrete patio, under the aluminum awning. He scanned the small side yard from broken sidewalk to weathered wooden fence. There was nothing at first, but then he saw them.

Scattered all over the place were tiny figures. What they were at first wasn't clear, so he bent over and picked one up. The breath sucked right out of his body when he saw what they were.

He quickly sucked in air and ran out to the street to see if there were any cars around, but he didn't see anyone. Whoever had littered the yard with tiny plastic mermaids was long gone.

Jake felt himself freaking out a little bit. This seemed so out of the blue, so bizarre. but then his mind went back to the strange guy standing in the parking lot last night. His comments at the time seemed a little off, but now it just seemed downright peculiar.

Jake didn't even know what to think. He wanted to run to the beach and talk to Ariel, but chances were she wouldn't be there. In fact, he knew she wouldn't. For some reason he felt compelled to start picking up all the tiny figures. He ran around the yard collecting them, dropping them into a steel bucket that used to hold a small pine tree at one time but was now just home to a small amount of rocks and dirt.

When they were all collected, he took the bucket and dropped it next to the dilapidated old shed in the back of the house. A sigh of relief escaped him and he didn't even know why. It's not like a bunch of little plastic mermaids would mean anything to anyone else but him.

After going back inside, the one thought that kept sticking to him was that she was real. He knew it already after last night, but now that someone else obviously knew, it became even more real. His fantasy and his reality had just collided. She was real, and someone was trying to scare him away from her.

He quickly dressed and headed to his car. There was no way she was going to be there, but he drove to the beach at Fort Fisher anyway. It was going to be a wasted trip, there was no doubt, but he needed to try.

Sure enough, after climbing the rocks, and scanning the ocean, Ariel was nowhere to be seen. He called out to her several times, but she didn't show up. He went back to his car in frustration, about to head back home, when he recalled something he'd seen the other day.

Mashing the gas pedal to the floor, he sped up the road to the quirky roadside stand where he'd see the picture of the mermaid on the wall. The place was closed this early in the morning so he just sat in the parking lot and waited.

At some point, he must have fallen asleep. Awoken abruptly by the slamming of a car door, he sat up. The sun had risen and the cluttered roadside storefront was bathed in bright light and a few curious tourists.

Tourist season was in full swing and the beaches were crawling with people, mostly from all points north and west. Jake was used to them after years of living at the beach. He liked the town better when they were all gone, but he didn't really mind it when they were here, either. Some Wilmington area locals begrudged the tourists, but he didn't care. He just went about his day dealing with the extra traffic.

Walking around the store, however, he wished they were gone because he didn't want to deal with them at the moment. He waited patiently, walking around the random items on the warped steel shelves, the pieces of old furniture and other oddities, not really looking at anything in particular, but glancing up continuously at the mermaid picture.

The crusty old beach bum behind the counter eyed him, probably worried he was trying to steal something, but Jake just stayed the course and walked around.

A tourist family of four started to filter out of the store and Jake moved up to the counter. He studied the picture past the shopkeeper's shoulder, trying to figure out if it was Ariel, but it wasn't clear enough. It was grainy and low resolution.

"You like that picture." The man's voice was scratchy. He had a long gray ponytail, thick gray goatee, and a black seashell necklace.

Jake nodded. "What's the story behind it?"

The man leaned forward. "That there's one of the only shots you'll ever see of the Emerald Cove mermaid."

"Huh?"

"You're a local. I recognize you."

Jake nodded. "Yeah."

"I've seen you out, you work at the bike shop on the island."

Jake nodded. "I did, yeah." He didn't want to mention that he owned the place but stopped paying his rent after the accident.

The man looked around. "You ain't never heard of the Emerald Cove mermaid?"

"No. I've never even heard of Emerald Cove. Should I have?"

"Well, there ain't really an Emerald Cove, but there used to be a restaurant by that name over near the river side at Snow's Cut. It fell down in a hurricane way back."

"Never heard of it."

The man stuck out his hand. "Name's Ridge."

"Good to meet you, Ridge."

"You still surf?"

"Yeah."

"Grab yer stick and meet me at CB south in twenty. I'll be just past access twenty-six."

Jake nodded and exited the building without a word.

* * *

After sliding his surfboard off the roof rack of his car, Jake traversed across the soft sand to the water. He saw Ridge bobbing about a hundred feet from the shoreline. The waves were not very large, so there weren't any other surfers out there. A few skimboarders and swimmers frolicked to his left, but otherwise it wasn't a busy beach afternoon in the breakers.

He labored past a few slappy swimmers and an old man on a body-boarder, but when he pulled up, sat next to Ridge, and looked back at the shore, he remembered how much he missed this.

Ridge looked back behind. "Kinda flat."

Jake glanced. "Yeah, not much to speak of."

"Sometimes I just come out and sit for an hour. Even if I don't catch a wave I like the motion of the sea. It's in my soul."

"I know what you mean." Jake nodded.

Ridge looked at him. "It's in your soul too. It's in your eyes. Every surfer I've ever met has that look in their eyes. It's a twinkle that comes up from the soul and vibes out into the world. It says, *hey man, I get it*, and most people don't."

Jake nodded. "I feel like that's probably true."

"The ocean is a way of life. It's something in the salty air, it just pulls you in and melts into you. I could never live inland. The sea is in me."

"Yeah, I know what you mean. And it's not the same up north, either."

"No sir. It is not."

"I lived in New York City for four years in college. I went to NYU. It was not an ideal situation."

"The ocean is not the same up there, no Gulf Stream. It smells different, feels different. Once you get into the subtropical moisture everything changes for the better."

"I guess so."

Ridge took a deep breath and blew it out. "Why'd you wander into my shop?"

Jake looked down into the water. "The mermaid picture…who took it?"

"You're looking at him."

"When?"

"Twenty-five years ago this summer."

"She was real."

Ridge looked at him and narrowed his eyes. "You bet your ass she was real."

"Was?"

"At some point you have to let go. I never saw her again after that week."

"You saw her for a week?"

"Yes, sir, one glorious week."

"You spoke with her?"

Ridge sighed. "Sometimes things we want to remember just aren't there for our brains to pull up. That was a long time ago, in another life, another world."

Jake looked up at the shore. "I've seen her."

Ridge nodded. "I know. But what you're seeing is not what I saw."

"How do you know?"

Ridge started paddling out deeper toward a small budding set of waves.

Jake yelled. "How do you know?"

Ridge turned. "There's something you need to see." He caught the momentum, jumped up on his board, and rode the wave.

Jake waited a second for the next wave in the set and paddled in. At that perfect moment he'd learned through years of practice, he popped up on his board, a perfect landing.

The wave wasn't much to speak of, it was slow and small, and probably a good wave for a beginner to get a feeling on. But it was the first wave he'd snagged in months and it felt pretty damn good.

76

As the ride neared its end, he kicked up the nose and dropped backwards into the water.

* * *

Back at the shop, Ridge led him down into the basement, via some old rickety wooden stairs. The basement had a concrete floor and was packed wall to wall with all sorts of things. Jake had never seen so much useless junk. "Do you sell a lot of this stuff?"

Ridge ducked his lanky frame under a hanging net. "You'd be surprised what these tourists will buy."

"I probably would."

"I sell them bottles of sand with shells in it. It says Carolina Beach on the glass, but it's made in China."

"Of course."

"Thing is, I used to sell actual sand from CB, but the tourists pay more for the crappy China sand because it had fancy writing on the glass. They pay twice as much and it costs me half as much. And after all, I'm in business to make money."

He made his way to the back of the basement, where an old non-operating chest freezer sat. Ridge removed a few boxes of junk from atop the old silver chest, and opened the heavy lid. "I saved the newspaper clippings." He handed Jake an old newspaper. "That paper went out of print about fifteen years ago."

Jake looked at the front cover. It wasn't anything remarkable. "What am I looking at?"

"Turn to page six."

Jake flipped the tabloid style paper to page six. The headline read:

Body of Woman Found on Beach.

Jake went on to read aloud, "The body of an unidentified woman found on Carolina Beach this past Saturday, is not that of missing local woman Sharon Royce, missing since August. As of this printing, the body was still unidentified. An autopsy is scheduled for this week in Wilmington. Police did acknowledge the woman had extensive damage to her lower extremities but would not elaborate."

Ridge handed him another paper. "Intrigued yet?"

Jake took hold of the other paper. It had another unimpressive front page. "What page?"

Ridge pointed. "Page eight."

Jake thumbed through until he saw the article with the headline,

Body of Woman Still a Mystery.

"The body of the woman who washed up on the beach last month is still unidentified. Blah-blah-blah…huh. It says medical examiner Dorian Friedberg determined the cause of death was a small caliber gunshot wound to the head. He also confirmed that the woman had extreme abnormalities to the lower part of her body." Jake looked to Ridge. "Extreme abnormalities?"

"Indeed."

"What does that mean?"

"It gets better." He handed Jake another paper. "Turn to page three."

He flipped to page three and dropped open his jaw. "C'mon. Seriously?"

"Read it."

"Police confirmed that three bodies were stolen from the Wilmington medical examiner's office last night and a security guard was assaulted. One of the bodies stolen was that of the unidentified woman found on Carolina Beach on August sixth. Police have no leads and are looking for information on the incident."

Ridge made a hand gesture. "Poof."

"You think that woman was the woman you took the picture of?"

"I know it was. I was on the beach when they found the body."

"Didn't everyone see the mermaid tail?"

Ridge shook his head sadly. "It had been severely mutilated. No one knew what they were looking at. Even I wasn't sure and I'd seen her."

"So who took the body?"

Ridge turned a frown. "Probably the same sonofabitch that mutilated her. Or maybe some government agency. Someone doesn't want us to know about something. They tried to scare us away." He waved a hand. "Ah, who the hell knows, man? It's all bad news. It don't even matter who took her."

Jake made a face. "Why are you telling me this?"

"You kinda remind me of a younger me. I know that look in your eyes of having seen something that you can't decide is real. And you can't decide if you want it to be real or not, and that's the scary part. Admitting it's real makes you crazy. Admitting it's not real makes you crazier. You're damned if you do and damned if you don't."

Jake read something in his face. "You saw her more than one week, didn't you?"

Ridge nodded once. "We see what we want to see, when we want to see it."

Jake took a step toward him. "Someone doesn't want me to see her again."

"Then let it go, son. You don't want to chase the squirrel up that tree…nothing but briers up there."

"Did you let it go?"

Ridge looked at him but didn't reply.

"You let it go and she still wound up dead. Didn't she?"

Ridge snarled a tooth at him. "I think you need to leave now."

Jake read his face and didn't want to push it. He sighed and turned away. Before he got to the steps, he turned back. "I appreciate your help."

Ridge nodded. "Just fair warning, bro. Let it go away and it will. If you go down that road, you might not like where it leads."

Jake turned back and headed up the steps.

Chapter 11

Jake entered the pawnshop with the last few pieces of jewelry. He had to buy a few things and this was his last hope to raise the cash.

As he approached the counter, an older woman with short red hair approached him. "Hi, sweetie, what can we do for you today?" She had a measurable southern accent.

Jake placed the ring, bracelet, and necklace on the counter. "I want to sell these."

The woman quickly looked over the things. "These aren't stolen, are they?" She chuckled.

"No, they aren't."

"I'm just kidding, honey. I've seen you in here before." She performed a few tests on the gold and diamonds. "These are nice things."

"They probably weren't cheap."

"Buy 'em for a girl, did ya?"

"Actually, they were given to me by my grandparents. They got them in Europe. I was supposed to give them to someone."

"Aha, wedding things for a wedding that didn't

happen. We see that a lot."

"Yeah, I just…I have no reason to keep them now."

"These are nice pieces. We'll give you a great price."

"I trust you."

After doing some calculations, she wrote three numbers on a piece of yellow paper and showed them to Jake. He moved his head back. "Are you kidding?"

She made a face. "Well, I can up it a little bit, but I think that's fair market price."

"No, I mean, that seems very generous."

"Well, they're expensive pieces. I'll go to the safe and get you a check. I can't give you cash for this much."

She gave Jake way more than he expected for the pieces. He had no idea this stuff was worth so much. He'd hoped to get a few thousand bucks or so…he didn't expect to get ten times that much. She said the ring would probably resell all by itself for six or eight thousand dollars.

On his way back from the bank he stopped by his shop. He still had the keys even though he had not paid his rent in months. With this money, he could definitely get the shop up and running again if he wanted.

He pushed open the glass door and flipped on the lights. The place still looked clean and ready for business. After the accident, he'd tried to come into work but could not. He and Paul were the only two people who worked in the shop full time. He hadn't known Paul very long, only about a year after he moved down from Michigan, but they became best buds. He was handy with a wrench and charismatic with the customers.

He also had a part-time kid who helped on weekends, but Jake let him go when he could not keep the shop running. Before the accident, profits were at an all-time high and climbing steadily. His projections were putting him so far into the black that he'd have enough business to hire at least one more full-time person and another two part-timers every summer. He'd just branched out into the bike rental aspect at the end of the summer and that promised to be very lucrative.

As he walked by rows of bikes and parts, he missed his everyday life for the first time since the accident. His visit was nostalgic in a way. It was like this place was frozen in time, stuck in the exact place he'd left his life.

He glanced up at his baseball trophies on the tall shelf above the register, and his mountain bike trophies below those. It had been a long time since he'd bothered to look at them. He was proud of them, but he was the only one. Neither of his parents were ever really present in his life, they were too busy messing up their own. As long as he stayed out of trouble so his mother's reputation would not be tarnished, that's all that mattered.

He gripped the bars on his favorite red bicycle. It sat untouched in the same place he'd left it. After a few more moments, he locked up and went back to his car, glancing once at the sign that had his name, *'Wheeler's Bikes,'* in red letters.

After heading back home to pick up his kayak,

he drove out to the inlet at Fort Fisher. Whoever sent him that warning to stay away from Ariel obviously didn't know him very well.

He dropped the boat in the shallows and quickly paddled out into the water, working hard to get away from the shore as fast as possible past the breakers. The waves were still small, but according to his surf report, they were going to pick up later. And this side of the island was not as choppy.

Once he settled into the calm, he took out his phone and started looking at the maps. There were numerous small islands and inlets around the area. One of them had to be the place where Ariel was retreating.

Cutting his oar into the water, he headed toward the closest series of islands. At first glance, none of them appeared to be large enough to house anything. But as he got deeper into the vegetation of the snaking inlet they got larger in size. On one of the farther ones was a house, brown, slat-board, dilapidated. It didn't look like anyone could live there. Maybe someone had fifty years ago.

Grounding the kayak onto the rocky shore with a few hard shoves, he climbed out and walked up the wet sand to the house. The place was deserted, and had been for a long time. He pressed on, opening the front door with a shove of his shoulder. The door protested and fought but he managed to twist inside.

The place smelled like the sea. The wood had soaked up years of salt and seaweed, but surprisingly the interior looked to be mostly intact. It was dirty, and musty, but it looked better than he figured it would.

It appeared that there was once an upstairs. But only the bones of the staircase remained and reached to nowhere. He looked straight up to the beamed roof. The place was too big to call a shack, but fell short of being a house at this point.

Jake moved cautiously over the wooden floor as the creaks and groans of protesting panels threatened to crack and drop him into the basement. Although a look through some of the busted planks revealed no basement, only a dirt crawlspace of about two feet down.

He felt like this was a waste of time but explored the island extensively anyway. He wasn't even sure why he was here…other than the peacefulness the place had nothing to offer. Nothing here was going to help him. The sun was dropping and he didn't want to get caught out there in the dark, so he decided to head back.

With a shove and a hop, he was back into the water and paddling out. As he cut around the first path back toward open water, he saw her on the rocks. For the first time, he saw her entire form, tail and all just lying there. She was on her side with her head propped on her hand.

"Ariel, I didn't expect to see you."

"What're you doing out here?"

"I was looking for you."

"So you did expect to see me."

Jake thought about her point. "I guess what I meant was I didn't expect to see you just right out in the open, it's still daylight. How'd you find me?"

"I had a feeling. I'm not exactly sure." She

smiled coyly. "I'm drawn to you, I guess. This place is very secluded. No one comes back here."

"But I just did."

Ariel smiled. "But no one else would be so nosy."

"I wanted to see you."

"Now you see me." She smiled. "And now you don't." With a splash she jumped into the water and took off down the stream toward the ocean.

Jake slapped his paddle into the water, ripping off a few quick strokes on one side before switching to the more traditional left-right swipes that propelled him forward. Ariel popped up in front of him and looked back, to see if he was chasing.

Out into the flat deeper water, away from the inlets, she disappeared again and didn't come back up. Jake stopped and looked around. After what seemed like a long wait, she popped up at the bow of his kayak, and held on.

"Now you see me again."

He looked around. It wasn't nearly dark enough. "Isn't it kind of light out?"

"So?"

"So someone down the shore over there could see you."

"Not unless they have a telescope. Besides, I'm on the other side of your boat. They can't see me."

"I guess not." He glanced around. "Ariel, you should know that someone doesn't want me to see you."

"Why do you say that?"

"Last night, there was this strange guy by my car. He said some strange stuff. Then this morning, well, someone threw like a hundred little plastic mermaids at my house."

She looked at him and for the first time her pretty smile seemed to sour. He'd never seen her look so serious. Yet she still looked so beautiful. She glowed even when she wasn't trying to glow. "What could it mean?"

"I don't know, Ariel. But obviously someone is trying to scare me away from you."

"You don't know that. And anyway, that's impossible. No one has seen us together."

He shrugged. "Someone has. I met someone today who said he saw someone like you, only a long time ago."

Ariel let her chin drop to her arms. She looked so sad.

"Hey," Jake said. "Don't be sad. I'm not afraid."

"There is no one like me anymore."

"But there was."

Ariel nodded. "Father told me she died."

"Your mother?"

She nodded as tears welled up in her eyes. "She died on the day I was born."

"I'm sorry."

"Don't be sorry, it's the circle of life. My kind must die in order to be born."

"What? Who told you that?"

"Father told me."

"That doesn't make any sense."

"That's the way it goes. Soon I will become pregnant and then I too will have to die."

"That's ridiculous. I don't believe that."

"It's all true."

"How can that be?"

"It has always been that way."

"That's morbid. That's sad."

"It's only sad to you. I've been ready for it my entire life."

Jake knew something was askew. If the woman that washed up on the beach twenty some years ago was Ariel's mother, she didn't die of natural causes. She died from a gunshot wound to the head.

"Ariel, what's your father's name?"

She looked at him as if no one had ever asked her and she didn't know the answer. She eventually replied. "His name is Bruce Shepard. Why do you ask?"

He was a little surprised he had a name. "I was just curious."

"You can't tell that to anyone, Jake, not a soul. I'm not even supposed to know that."

"Huh? Why aren't you supposed to know your own father's name?"

"That's just the way it is. We mermaids aren't supposed to know about our human guardians."

"Well, isn't he your father?"

"He's my guardian, he's not my father. I don't have a father."

"Well, forgive me for asking, but how did your mother get pregnant?"

"Mermaids just become pregnant when they hit a certain age. There is no partner needed for procreation."

"What?" Jake laughed a little. "This is so bizarre."

"There are many creatures of the sea who are

born with seed. And that seed takes many years to bloom. I will become pregnant when the time is right."

"So you never got to meet your mother, and you have no father."

"We lead lonely lives. The sea is our only friend."

"How do you get your human guardians?"

"They are chosen for us. We do not question these things."

"Ariel, I gotta say, I thought being a mermaid was the weirdest thing about you, but your whole deal is far more bizarre than I would've imagined."

"It is a unique life, but we cannot choose it. What we are born into are just the circumstances of our existence. We enjoy them to the best of our abilities."

"Every creature on earth should have free will. It should be a God given right."

"I have free will. I can freely enjoy my life for as long as it lasts, as limited as it is. I don't dwell on what might be or what could be, I only live in what is."

Jake didn't know what else to say. He could learn a lot from her. "I guess that's admirable."

"We grow where we are planted, Jake."

"Well, where you're planted sucks."

"Only to you. I do not wish to aspire to be more than I am."

He nodded, but her face hid another truth. It was getting dark and he didn't want to have to navigate back to the shore blind. "I have to start heading back."

"I will swim with you."

They coasted through the sea in silence for several minutes. Then Ariel said, "You're sad. I can sense it."

"I'm sad for you."

"Don't be."

"I'm trying not to be. But I'm also sad for me, selfishly."

"That's natural."

"I just met you, and now I feel like you're going to be taken away from me too. Just like everyone else."

"Not for a time still."

"So you say. But apparently you don't even know when you're going to have to die. This is a horrible uncertainty."

"I will have nine months to prepare myself for it."

"Birth is supposed to be beautiful, but for you it's a death sentence."

"Life is a death sentence, Jake. We are all born to die."

"That's just too depressing."

"It can be, but it can also be freeing. I live like my life is going to be short because it is. I enjoy every moment. I see the wonder everywhere. You should too." She popped up on the kayak with him and wrapped her arms around his neck. Then she kissed him long and soft, yet firm.

She let go and slid back into the sea. "Goodnight, sweet Jake. Sleep well and dream of the sea—dream of me—and in another universe—what we could be." And she slipped away.

Chapter 12

Carrying his kayak back to his car, he didn't expect to see Ashley waiting for him. "Ashley, what're you doing here?"

"I stopped by the house to see you. Tom said you'd taken the kayak, so I figured you were either at Masonboro or here."

He put down the plastic boat. "What's going on?"

She shrugged. "Not much. I just wanted to see a friendly face."

"Is everything okay on the home front?"

"Not so much really, no. Mike and I are not getting along and it's just getting worse all the time. It's becoming unbearable."

"What's wrong?"

"I don't even know. I think we're going to get a divorce. We just argue about everything lately. I'm just having a real hard time feeling good around him. I don't want to be around him at all. I'm going to see a lawyer on Monday."

"I'm really sorry."

"Yeah, well, don't get married." She put her hand over her gaping mouth. "I'm so sorry, Jake. That was insensitive of me. I can't believe I said that. I just slipped up. I forgot who I was talking to for a second."

"It's okay, Ash, really it is. I'm really doing so much better. I don't want you to have to edit yourself around me."

She smiled. "I'm happy to hear that. You have no idea."

"Well, a lot of that has to do with you. I think you should know that. I think you do know that."

She smiled. "I'm glad."

God he missed that quirky little smile. Ashley had a smile that could always send his heart soaring. Even in his deepest love with Cassie, seeing Ashley smile had a special feeling. He didn't know what it meant, if anything, but it was still there.

"Do you want to get a drink or something?"

She nodded. "I could use something."

"Lemme put the kayak back on my car. We'll just leave your car here."

"That's fine." She picked up half the kayak and helped him mount it on the roof of the Beetle.

They drove off.

"Where do you want to go?" Jake shifted gears as the road smoothed out.

"Let's go to the Tiki. We can sit on the pier and just listen to the waves while my brain turns into an alcoholic stew."

He nodded. "Sure, we can do that. But we may end up walking home."

"That's fine as long as we stay on the island to

drink."

"Ha, of course we would…where else would we go?"

"Well, we could go downtown."

He laughed and didn't see the car that had sped up and bumped softly into the rear of them. "Whoa!" Jake exclaimed.

Ashley turned around. "What the hell?"

The car bumped into them again, a little harder.

Jake's first reaction was to pull to the side of the road, and when he did, the car pulled up next to them unexpectedly. He didn't realize what he was seeing until the cracking sound of gunfire tore into the night.

He hit the gas hard, sending them lurching forward. He glanced over at Ashley to make sure she wasn't hurt. "You okay?"

"Fine, just get us the hell out of here."

Jake had always been a top end driver, which was part of the thing that bothered him so much about the accident. He should have been able to drive his way out of it like he always had before.

But right now he wanted to get away from the threat. He cut the wheel hard, grabbed the emergency brake, and sent the Beetle into quick 180-degree spin. Then he mashed the gas pedal and sent the car screeching forward. Thank goodness this was a modern age turbo-charged Beetle with a good amount of giddy-up and go, not one of the old clunkers, or they'd be doomed. It just looked like an old clunker, but it ran well.

Their pursuer turned around with screeching tires and hurried toward them again. He thought he heard more bullets but wasn't sure. The engines and tires and twisting of machinery was impossible to discern.

Jake cut the wheel again, did another 180-degree turn, and headed straight at the car charging at them.

"Jake, what're you doing?"

"Trust me."

Ashley reached up and grabbed the plastic handhold on the A-pillar. She gripped it for dear life. Jake drove straight at the oncoming car full speed, and at the last second cut the wheel so hard the car nearly rode up on two wheels. He cut the wheel back onto the road and just kept the gas pedal pinned, heading up the beach road toward the more populated areas. He looked up one more time in the rearview mirror and saw the chaser peel off down one of the side streets. Whoever they were thought better of the chase into the busy areas.

He pulled into the busy boardwalk and shut off the car. They sat in silence while they caught their breath.

Ashley looked over to him. "What the hell was that, Jake?"

He shook his head. Not a single part of him wanted to tell her the story, but every single part of him knew he had to. If there was anyone on this planet he had to trust right now, it had to be Ashley. He could kid himself and say it had nothing to do with Ariel, but he knew that was a lie.

"Okay, Ashley, I'm about to tell you a story. You're going to think I'm crazy, I'm sure of it. But you have to trust me it's all real."

"You're freaking me out a little bit."

"Well, this is some weird shit."

"You can tell me anything, you know that."

Jake went on in detail about everything. He told the story from the first night he'd seen Ariel while he held a gun to his head, to the last conversation they'd just had tonight and everything in between. He'd left out only one part, the part about the kisses. That was one detail he didn't need to share. He watched her face the entire time, trying to pick out at what point she assumed he'd lost his mind, but she had a good poker face.

Finally, when he was done he sat back into the seat, waiting for her response. She sighed and just said, "Let's go get that drink."

After a short walk across the boardwalk to Hurricane Alley, they slid up to the wooden bar. They ordered some strong drinks and downed them, then Jake looked at her and asked, "Are you going to say something?"

She looked at him. "Jake, I don't know what to say. And I'm not being funny. I literally don't know *what* to *say*. I mean, I thought you were doing so well, and now I want to think you're cracking up."

"That's fair."

"Are you cracking up?"

"No, Ashley, I'm not. I haven't been this lucid in months."

"I just don't...I mean...what would you say to someone who told you that stuff?"

He shrugged. "I'd say they were nuts."

"Right? I mean, what else could it be?"

He downed the shot in front of him. "That guy

with the gun in the car wasn't an illusion."

Ashley downed her shot of whiskey. "Well, I know, Jake, but that's easier to believe than some sort of crazy mermaid conspiracy." She laughed. "I mean, next thing you're going to tell me is that you're in love with her."

Jake didn't answer right away. Ashley took that as a yes.

"Oh, come on, Jake, don't even."

"No, I'm not in love with her. I'm intrigued by her."

"That seems to be like the same thing right now."

"I wish I could explain it but here we are. And she's real."

She took another drink and asked for another. Then after a few minutes, she looked at him and said, "Okay, let's play. Maybe this is all real. What does it mean?"

"I don't know what it means."

"I'm sorry, Jake—I can't wrap my head around this."

"Ashley, do you trust me?"

She looked at him, met his eyes. "You know I do."

"Then believe."

"I want to."

"Then do it."

She sipped the pineapple-spiked rum the bartender placed on front of her. "Okay, Jake. I'm going to trust you. You've seen something out of this world. I will believe you."

"Thank you."

"But you have to give me some leeway here to doubt a little bit. Okay?"

"Okay."

"I do trust you, and that's the *only* reason I'm willing to bend my belief in reality."

"The world is a strange place."

"Yeah, but I don't believe in any of it. I believe in things I've seen. And I'm sorry, but I've never seen a ghost, or a UFO…or a mermaid."

"Just because you haven't seen it doesn't mean it's not real."

"That's fair."

"Someone tried to kill us, Ashley. We didn't imagine that."

"I can't argue with that, but for all I know that has nothing to do with any mermaid." She gulped her drink again. "I've never been shot at before."

"It was a first for me too."

"I don't even want to go back and get my car."

"We can get it in the morning."

"Mike is going to flip his plugs."

Jake chuckled, feeling a little tipsy. "He's got plugs?"

She laughed. "He started going bald at like twenty-five."

"Somehow that seems like karma."

She gave him a look. "How come you never liked Mike?"

"He's a big flapping douche bag." They laughed.

"No really."

Jake shrugged. "I don't know exactly. He always just rubbed me the wrong way. He's kind of a dork but he thinks he's cool. He thinks he's smarter than everyone but not in a professor-y kinda way. More like, in an I'm a rich guy so by default I'm better than you kinda way. He acts like an Alpha male but he's really not."

"He rubs a lot of people the wrong way. But what was it specifically?"

"Well, I guess at that time I didn't think he was good enough for you."

"At that time? Why?" She flashed a coy smile.

"I think you know."

She smiled at him and just shook her head.

"You're going to make me say it."

She smiled and nodded.

"Fine, and you know this already, so you're just acting dumb. But I had feelings for you."

"And you felt guilty."

"I always did because I was supposed to be in love with Cassie."

"You mean Cassie?"

"What did I say?"

"You said Cassie."

"Huh?"

She laughed. "I'm screwing with you."

"I hate you."

"No, you don't."

Jake nodded. "No, I do not." Jake looked at his drink and wondered if he was feeling drunk already. Now that the adrenaline was fading, the drinks he just downed in record time were hitting him hard.

"You were in love with Cassie."

"I know I was. I really was. But it always bothered me. I always felt that if I was so in love with Cassie, if everything was so perfect, how could

I fall in love with someone else?"

"Life isn't perfect, Jake. We make choices and time goes by, and we struggle with the decisions all our lives. Sometimes what we have we don't want, and what we want we can't have."

"It wasn't even about wanting what I didn't have. I had it." He looked at her more directly. "It was just you more than anything else. You just got me, more than anyone I'd ever met before. We had some unspoken connection that just locked me up."

"That's fair."

"Did you feel it?"

"Jake, are you kidding me? Of course I felt it. But what was I going to do about it? You were freshly engaged to be married. I was already married. What was there to do?"

He shrugged. "I don't know. Sometimes I wish I'd thrown it all away just to be with you."

"Remember that night?"

"The aloe plant?"

"Yes, with the aloe plant. How come you didn't kiss me?"

"I told you, I didn't want to be that guy."

"Really? Is that the only reason?"

He searched his feelings and sighed. "No, that's not the only reason."

"What was it?"

He blew out a long breath. "I didn't want to ruin what we had. But most importantly, I didn't want you to be the *other* woman…I wanted you to be the *only* woman."

Ashley's face flushed. She brought her hands up to her face and ran her fingers through her hair.

"Jake, what're you doing to me?"

"What?"

She emptied her drink and slammed it on the bar. "That was one of the most heartfelt, romantic, beautiful things anyone ever said to me."

"I'm sorry?"

"Don't be sorry. I'm just…it just couldn't have come at a more impossible time. I mean, we're being shot at, you tell me you're in love with a mermaid, me and Mike are one inch away from visiting a lawyer and dividing our things. My head is just a mess right now and then you hit me with that."

"It was a long time ago, Ashley. We're not the same people we were. We've done a lifetime of growing up since then."

"Is that what you tell yourself?"

He shrugged. "It's the truth."

"The truth is an illusion, Jake. We make the truth up as we go along."

"I don't make the truth up, I just speak it. Some people can't handle that, some people want to think it's easier to lie. But that's not me. I have no instinct to lie or conceal the truth. I speak what I feel."

"Maybe you shouldn't."

"Trust me, I know. People claim they want honesty and truth, but really they don't. They like the security of their lies. They like the illusions and the fantasy and the games. The moment things are real they run away scared, like immature little babies."

"Not everyone and not all the time."

"I guess I've struggled with it all my life." He

downed another drink.

"So, you don't feel that way about me anymore?"

He shrugged. "I don't know what I feel anymore."

She played with a coaster. "Maybe you should figure that out."

He looked away and let his eyes fall on the stuffed monkey on the wall. "I guess maybe I should."

Chapter 13

Castro

Castro knocked on the door of the office. When the short, thin, graying man opened the door, he gave Castro a hard look well beyond his physical prowess.

"You're late."

"I had car trouble."

He went to his desk and pulled out a small, black leather shoulder bag. "Here's the money. Thanks for your services."

"There're two problems."

"Yeah, what's that? My boss doesn't like problems."

"The first problem is that the job didn't get done."

"What? Oh, that's not going to sit well for either of us."

"Probably not. I tried to tell you on the phone but you insisted I come here and talk to you. But that's only one problem. I'm good at my job, so I will follow through and make it right."

"Okay, so what's the other problem?"

"You've seen me." Castro pulled a gun and shot the man in the heart.

He calmly holstered his pistol and walked out of the office. As he walked down the hallway, he dialed his phone. "One out of two jobs are done."

"Which one is done?"

"Your finance friend."

"But not the other one?"

"There was a complication."

"When do you expect it to be done?"

Castro exited the elevator and went through the lobby of the apartment complex. "I'm hoping later tonight we will be able to close the deal."

There was a long hesitation on the other end of the phone. "I want to be cautious here. This one seems smart. And she seems especially smitten. I don't want to move too quickly and force us into an unnecessarily hasty series of moves."

"Understood."

"So make sure you're extra careful. We can't have anything come back to us. This is a very critical juncture for us."

"Understood."

"It's been a long while. I just want to make sure we're smart."

"Understood. But know that it's only been a while for you. You're not my only client."

"Very well. Did you get your pay?"

"I did."

"Call me when you have an update."

"Understood." He ended the call.

Working for this particular corporation had always been a bit tricky. They required a certain amount of tact because the nature of their business was so sensitive. This was not nearly the most sensitive work he'd done. Protecting secrets was what he did, it was his main income. Keeping the secrets was what kept him employed with various firms. He'd dealt with matters of global security on a regular basis, things that if they got out would change the entire scope of humanity. So working for this firm, which he had done several times in the past, was kind of like a holiday with pay.

This particular target made him feel a little cautious for some reason. That had never happened. There was something about the situation. He could not put his finger on it, but it was bothersome. Extra caution might be in order.

Chapter 14

Jake

Jake pulled into Ashley's driveway. He didn't normally drive with a buzz, but he let it fade quite a bit before getting in the car. And they only had to go two miles on a deserted back street. "What're you going to tell Mike about the car?"

"I'm just going to tell him I was too drunk to drive."

"Is that better? I mean, it's one-thirty in the morning and some guy is dropping you off all drunk."

"What options are there? He's going to know I'm drunk."

"You could tell him the car broke down."

She shrugged. "Why lie? Nah, if he can't take the truth, screw him. At this point it doesn't even matter anyway. I'm just going to sleep in one of the guest bedrooms."

"Okay. It's your call."

"What about you?"

Jake frowned. "What *about* me?"

"You okay?

"I'm fine."

"I'm worried about you driving that far."

"Why?"

"Why? Because someone fired a gun at us and whoever did that might come back."

"Yeah, they might." Jake didn't want to show he was worried. But it had just occurred to him he doesn't even have a gun anymore.

"Maybe you should stay here tonight. You can sleep downstairs."

Jake didn't want to accept the offer. He didn't need the drama of Mike starting something. "I don't know, that's not really necessary. I'm not that buzzed anymore."

"It may not be necessary, but it's smart."

"I don't know."

"I do." She reached over, grabbed the keys in the ignition, turned the car off, and got out. "Now you've got no choice."

Jake sighed as he watched her head up the driveway with his keys. She turned back, jingled them, and said, "C'mon, Jake, you're not sleeping in the car."

He reluctantly got out and caught up with her by the front door. "Mike's not going to like this."

"I don't care."

He stopped her at the door. "I do. I don't want to get into the middle of anything with you two."

"You won't." She poked her key into the lock. "He's not confrontational in front of other people. Besides, there's nothing left to get in the middle of."

"If you say so."

"He's a pussy. He knows I'd kick his ass if he started some shit." She opened the door and they went inside.

Jake had been in this house before but it looked so much nicer than he recalled. The kitchen was large, and granite counter tops and stainless steel appliances dominated the space. "The place looks good."

"It had better. We spent over twenty thousand redoing the kitchen alone."

"Whoa." They moved into the living room, which was equally impressive with its expensive hardwood floors and marble fireplace.

"Impressive, huh?"

"I guess I forgot how much money Mike makes."

"Oh, he makes a ton. I don't have to work if I don't want to. He wants me to stay home and have babies."

"That doesn't sound like you."

"It's not."

She led him through the living room, toward some French doors that led to the patio. The guest room was to the right. She opened the door. "It's all yours. I'll see you in the morning."

"I thought you wanted to sleep in the guest room?"

"There's another three bedrooms upstairs. I'll sleep on the futon in the study."

He walked past her, and she hugged him. It was a strange hug. It was not a friendly hug. It was more. It lingered. It was tight, close.

With his words unfit for release, he managed to squeak out, "Thanks Ash, for everything."

She whispered softly. "What're friends for?"

"I feel like you've gone above and beyond."

They were cheek-to-cheek, and he felt the heat of her exhale. For a moment, he was back in time to that night, that one amazing moment that he wasted, that one moment of regret that he never thought he'd get another chance at. He desperately wanted to kiss her. Their lips were only an inch away, he felt the gooseflesh on her arm, he could taste her breath but she pulled away ever so slowly. Their lips did not meet.

"Sleep well."

He sucked a deep breath. "Goodnight."

She closed the door and he settled on top of the blankets, only kicking off his sneakers. He still had a slight buzz from the alcohol and he felt the spin when on his back. He probably shouldn't even have driven. He was not drunk by any stretch, but he could have waited another hour to sober up a bit more. The fact he did not eat anything probably didn't help.

He heard some hushed voices filtering down to his room, probably through the air ducts, one of which sat right above his head. He tried not to listen but couldn't really help it. Not all the words were clear but the gist of the conversation, as expected, was about Ashley being out so late, coming home drunk, and bringing a sad sack friend home with her. He wondered if they would even sleep in the same bed and when he heard two doors slam, he had his answer.

Jake closed his eyes and waited for some sleep to come. It always came easy but staying asleep was another problem. He'd usually wake up in two hours with his brain unable to shut down enough to fall back to sleep. So, when he fell asleep he wasn't surprised. He was even less surprised when he woke up two hours later and couldn't fall back to sleep.

Lying there thinking of everything and nothing at the same time was exhausting. Usually he would fall back to sleep after about an hour or so, but tonight felt like one of those nights that would be a struggle. The unfamiliar sounds of the house weren't helping. Strange creaks and pops were keeping him awake. Maybe the fact someone had shot a gun at him was keeping him extra vigilant, which was why he sat straight up in the bed when he heard the next noise.

Searching for his sneakers with his feet on the floor, he got up and slid his toes into the well-worn shoes. Padding softly, he went to the bedroom door and listened again just to make sure he wasn't hearing things.

The sound of breaking glass is very distinct. And although it was very faint, he swore he'd heard it. Now something more ominous was prevalent, the soft sound of slow steps on a wood floor. The creaks and shuffle were almost imperceptible, and would have been had he not been awake already. At first thought, he figured it was Mike or Ashley, but something inside him knew better. His intuition felt abuzz with needles.

This was getting ridiculous. If someone was

trying to rub him out, he wasn't going quietly. That irony was not escaping him. Just a few days ago, he was ready to kill himself, now he was ready to fight for his life.

But it wasn't just his life in danger now, he'd put Ashley and Mike in danger too. Whoever was creeping through their house was probably just as likely to kill them. He had to do something.

A quick look around the room didn't really reveal anything in terms of weaponry. The only thing that looked decent was a large umbrella. He silently slid the black and red rain shield out of the wicker basket near the television stand and gripped it tightly.

He wished he knew the house better, to know where the walker was in relation to this door. Busting out too soon would likely lead to his demise, too late would ruin his chances to get a good shot. The only thing he had on his side was the element of surprise because an umbrella wasn't really going to cut it against a gun.

Jake could hear his pulse coursing through his ears with each frantic heartbeat. With a deep breath, he twisted the door handle achingly slow and held it while listening. He kept his breath pent up in his lungs, and when he heard the next pop of the floor, he yanked the door open.

Ready to swing on anyone near him, there was nothing there. That's when he realized the noise was above his head. He swore under his breath and moved slowly toward the steps.

Trying to split the difference between silence and speed, Jake moved across the floor, exhaling when he got to the tile. He started up the stairs, stopping on every riser to listen to the sounds. It was quiet.

Onto the next step, he crept upwards and then the rustling, thump, scrape, scream, and the gunshots all smashed together in a string of sound.

Jake broke into a full-blown sprint up the steps, taking them two at a time. A few steps down the hall and he was right in the room. He slammed his body into the dark figure as another gunshot popped, lighting up the black room.

The man he'd hit was bigger, he smelled of musk and cigarettes. Jake took him down but bounced off when they hit the floor. Ashley's voice filled the darkness and her shadowy figure cast into the swatch of light that spilled into the room from the streetlights.

Jake saw the gun in the man's hand and went after it, trying to get some control on where the next shot might go. He yanked it hard, and much to his surprise, the man let go, causing him to scramble for his balance. He fell to his knees as the man punched him in the face. The assailant then threw Ashley across the room. She slammed hard into the heavy dresser and slid down to the floor. Jake fumbled for the handle on the gun but it fell to the floor. He reached down to grab it. The man crushed his hand with a stomping foot. Jake yelled in pain but spun away with a roll. He got to one knee but the man was gone.

Jake got up and was going to chase but stopped short; instead he went to Ashley to see if she was okay. "Ashley?" She was unresponsive other than a moan.

He stood upright and went after the attacker, gun in hand. Down the stairs, he trampled with thunderous noise, but his heart eclipsed it all. He got outside, hot on the heels of the figure, but the man was already across the grass and into the door of the blue sedan.

Jake got to the car just as the engine fired up and tore away from the curb. He had no recourse to stop it. He wanted to fire the gun but thought better of that, as there were too many houses around and a stray shot could be deadly. He watched helplessly as the car disappeared into the night with no lights on.

He stood there, unable to make a decision on what to do. As he turned to head back across the lawn, the sirens wailed in the near distance. Someone must have called about the shots. He jogged across the yard toward the front door, but the cop car was there in a second and they only knew one thing, he had the gun.

The car skidded to a stop, the officer jumped out with gun drawn. "Stop freeze! Drop the gun."

Jake quickly tossed the gun on the ground and stepped back with his hands up.

Chapter 15

Jake didn't like sitting handcuffed in an interview room, but he was just glad the cops didn't shoot him. After all, they rolled up onto a scene with him holding a gun. He was a little freaked out right now because he didn't know what had happened to Ashley or Mike. For all he knew, they were both dead.

Finally, when an older, gray-haired detective came into the room he felt a little better. At least he'd have some information.

"Jake, I'm Detective Bellamy. I just want to know what happened from your side."

"What happened?"

"That's what I want to know."

"Are Ashley and Mike okay?"

"What do you think?"

"I don't know. You arrested me before I could find out."

The detective smiled. "You're not the first man to kill his lover's husband, Jake. There's nothing to be embarrassed or afraid of. Love is a crazy powerful emotion."

Jake winced. "Mike is dead?" He shook his head. "Oh, God. This is my fault. Is Ashley okay?"

"Just tell me how it happened. Did he bust in on you with his wife?"

Jake shook his head. "What the hell are you talking about? I didn't kill anyone. I didn't kill Mike. A guy broke into the house. I tried to stop him."

"So a strange man broke into the house, and killed your lover's husband?"

"Ashley is not my lover, she's my friend. I was sleeping in the guest room downstairs."

"We performed a GSR, a gunshot residue test on you, we told you that will tell us if you shot a gun recently."

"Then you'll see I didn't. I never fired a single shot."

The detective looked at him. "Well, for your sake, I hope not. But we will know."

"And you'll see I didn't shoot anyone. Is Ashley okay?"

The detective stared at him for probably thirty straight seconds. He didn't look away. Then he said, "Yes, Ashley is okay. She took a hard shot to the head, a few stitches, but she's fine. She's being interviewed by my partner at the hospital right now."

Jake sighed. "Thank God."

"Why were you at the house?"

"Ashley invited me. We'd had an experience earlier and we were worried about our safety."

Detective Bellamy answered his AC/DC ring

tone. "Yeah...all right, okay." There was a long few minutes of silence. Then the detective finally said. "Okay, good work. As long as you have confirmation. All right, okay, uh-huh." He hung up the phone. "Well, Mr. Wheeler, it seems Miss Robertson confirmed you didn't shoot Mike. And she said something about you two being shot at earlier."

"I was going to tell you."

"We have to follow the laws of probability."

"I know."

"Why didn't you call us after you were shot at?"

Jake looked up. "I don't know. I guess that was stupid."

"Very stupid."

"I'm sorry, I should have." Jake leaned forward in the chair. "Can I go now? I need to go see Ashley."

"Yes, you're free to go." The detective unlocked his cuffs.

Jake got up and took a few steps. "Can I get a ride back to Ashley's house to get my car?"

"Actually your car is going to have to be taken into evidence for the shooting incident earlier. Miss Robertson filed an official report."

"But I don't think any bullets hit it."

"You don't think. But you don't know."

"I guess."

"We'll have it back to you by the end of the day."

"Then can you take me to my house so I can get my motorcycle?"

The detective passed a curious look, but then

agreed.

* * *

After one of the uniformed cops dropped him off at home, Jake went inside to find his helmet.

"Dude?" Tom stepped toward him as he entered the living room. Reaching out with his hands in stop position, Tom asked, "What happened? I heard some crazy shit."

"Yeah, bro…some crazy shit."

"Is Mike Robertson really dead?"

"Apparently."

"You killed him?"

"No, man—c'mon, why would you believe that?"

"I heard from Rizzo. He was down at Mako's with Peach and Rip, said one of his cop friends told him you were busted down for murdering that real estate guy. So I'm like what real estate guy, and Rizz said that Mike Robertson guy with his face all over Wilmington, and I was like, no way."

"No, I didn't kill him." He started looking for his helmet as Tom followed him around.

"So what happened?"

"Some dude busted into the house and shot him."

"Gnarly."

"Hey, have you seen my street lid?"

Tom ran his hands over his head in thought. "Oh yeah, it's in my room. I used your bike the other day."

"Did you put gas in it?"

"Sure did, bruh, full tank."

116

Jake retrieved his blue and yellow helmet and headed outside to remove the tarp from his red Honda sport. His bike wasn't fancy, or fast. But it was reliable, comfortable, and got about 60-plus miles to the gallon. He didn't mind if Tom used it as long as he replaced the gas, which he usually did.

With a flick of his thumb, the bike was running and he was off down the road. The air was hot inside the helmet. Today was a sun-drenched summer scorcher. The ride to the hospital was good. It cleared his mind. He'd ridden his bike a lot after the accident; it felt safer than getting into a car again for a long time. It was a very slim chance he was going to kill someone while he was on his bike, even if he'd done something stupid.

He parked, headed inside, and was about to walk up to the front desk when Ashley appeared from out of the silver elevators. Without a word, he went up and hugged her.

Finally, he pulled away. "Are you okay?"

She moved back into him and hugged him harder and longer. Her soft sobbing broke his heart. This was his fault. He may as well have pulled the trigger himself.

Ashley pulled back. "I didn't want him dead."

"I know you didn't."

"He was a pain in my ass, and I was going to divorce him, but I didn't want him dead."

"I know, Ash, I'm so sorry. This is my fault."

"It's not your fault, Jake. It's the psycho who broke into the house who's at fault."

"The cops thought I did it."

"I know." She wiped her tears with a tissue.

"They were certain you'd done it until I told them you didn't. Now they probably think we were both in on it."

"They do?"

"Not in so many words, but that lady detective was sort of suspicious of me. She hinted that they'd find whoever did this. And get this, she said, even if someone was hired to do it."

"Seriously?"

"I know, right?"

"They think we're lovers who wanted your husband out of the way."

"Pretty much."

"Well, let them investigate. We know the truth."

She wiped her tears with her palm. "What is the truth, Jake?"

He raked his teeth over his lip. "I told you the truth. You just don't want to believe it."

"Can you blame me?"

He sighed. "Maybe there's a way I can prove it."

They headed out to the bike. Jake unhooked the spare helmet and handed it to Ashley. "Oh—no." She waved her hand. "I'm not getting on that thing."

"Why not? I'm a great rider."

"I'm sure. I've just never been on one."

"You've never been on a bike?"

She snipped, "I feel like I just answered that question, Jake."

"Trust me." He swung his leg over the machine and held out his hand.

She reluctantly put the helmet on and got on behind him.

"Just hold on real tight," he said.

"You can count on that."

She gripped him tightly around the mid-section, and squeezed so hard he could barely breathe. "Not that tight."

"Sorry." She let up. "I'm just scared we're going to die."

"Relax. I've only crashed once and that was years ago."

"Oh God, you just jinxed us."

"Never." Jake headed out of the parking lot and into the Seventeenth Street traffic, quickly picking up speed. The squeal that came out of Ashley sounded like something between delight and fear. He wasn't sure which one until after a few minutes, her soft sounds started to seem more like exhilaration and less like terror.

They headed down the beach road, chasing the sun.

* * *

The cove beach wasn't busy. People were starting to make their way to their cars. The rocks were empty and the sunset was drawing near. Jake led Ashley up onto the boulders and picked a nice place to sit.

"Why're we here?" she asked. "We've wasted the entire afternoon."

"Wasted it?"

"Well, in a matter of speaking."

"You hate the bike."

Ashley smiled. "Okay, I have to admit I liked it a

lot."

Jake nodded to the ocean. "This is where I see her."

"Just like that, she just comes up to you?"

"Pretty much."

"Why?"

Jake looked out to the waves. The smell of the salt air calmed him. "For about three weeks, I came to this spot with a gun. Each night, I'd put it to my head."

"Jake." She touched his arm. "I didn't know you were that close. I mean, I'd heard you were…oh God." She put a hand to her chest. "I knew you were having a tough time, but holy shit, Jake. Were you really going to do it?"

"It was real bad. I was in a bad place. I didn't want to live anymore. I was going to do it. Technically, I shouldn't be here right now, and if not for her, I wouldn't be."

"I'm so sorry, Jake. I'm so sorry. I wish you'd've called me." She twisted to face him and wrapped her hands around both sides of his jaw, forcing him to look at her. "Why didn't you call me?"

"I couldn't call anyone, I was locked up. Then one night, I was finally about to pull the trigger…and Ariel showed up."

"That is horrible, Jake, I'm so sorry." Ashley pulled back. "Wait, her name is Ariel?" She chuckled. "I'm sorry. I shouldn't be laughing at you."

"I know it's ludicrous."

"A little bit…yeah." Ashley let her voice trail

120

off.

"That's part of the reason the first few times I saw her, I thought it was all in my head. I thought I was cracking up."

"Well, in fairness that still remains to be seen."

"Very funny. But she never comes out when anyone else is around, which was another thing that made me feel crazy."

"Why do you think she will now? Should I go hide?"

"I don't want you to. I want her to make the choice to introduce herself."

They waited in silence, letting the soft waves be the only sound for a long while. Jake then said, "I guess she's not going to come."

"I told you I should have hid."

"Maybe. I thought she'd trust me."

Just then, a familiar female voice said, "I trust you."

Jake stood and looked down over the last boulder. Ariel floated in the water with her elbows propped on the round wooden posts.

Ashley got up and let her jaw fall open. There was just enough light to see her body under the water. She moved a step to the edge of the rocks to get a better look, but remained speechless.

"Ariel," Jake said, "this is Ashley."

Ashley finally found her voice. "Oh, my God. Is this for real?"

Jake smiled. "Told you."

Ariel splashed her tail in and out of the water. "It's real."

"Ariel," Jake said. "Bad things are happening.

People are trying to kill us, and I think it's because of you. Remember what I told you about? Well, it's gotten worse."

She looked confused. "I don't understand. How could it be because of me?"

Jake shrugged. "I was hoping you could tell us."

Ariel twisted her face. "I haven't the faintest idea."

"Someone out there doesn't like me seeing you and they'll stop at nothing to make sure I don't again."

"But no one knows."

"Someone does."

Ariel sank underwater for a moment, then popped back up. "I don't know what it means."

"You have to think hard. There has to be someone."

"No one but you and Father even know I exist."

Jake blew out an audible breath. "That has to be it. Your father must know you've shown yourself to me."

"Impossible."

"It has to be him." He glanced over at Ashley, who continued to look at Ariel as if she was waiting for her to disappear.

Ariel huffed. "He wouldn't know. He doesn't follow me. No one does."

"Someone did." Jake quickly returned.

Ariel starred at him for a few long seconds. Then, "What do you think?" she looked at Ashley.

Ashley opened her mouth but didn't speak. She looked to be counting numbers in her head. Then in a distant voice she said, "I don't know what to think. I'm talking to a mermaid."

"It's not all that strange," Ariel offered. "The world is full of things that look strange to some but are common to others."

"Yeah," Ashley agreed, her voice restored. "But you're a mythical creature. This isn't supposed to be happening."

Ariel narrowed her eyes. "Be that as it may, I *am* a *creature*, I am here. Now what do you think about our problem?"

Ashley shook her head and looked at Jake. He lowered his head to her and she bucked up with an affirming nod. "I think Jake has a point. Someone knows about you showing yourself to him. And now you've shown yourself to me."

Ariel swam away from the shore a few strokes. "Do you see someone now?"

Jake and Ashley both looked around. He didn't see anyone, but the more he thought about it, the more he felt like he could have been being watched all the other times too. The darkness away from the beach was so absolute anyone could be lurking in those shadows. There was no way to know.

Jake wondered. "It's too dark to see if anyone's out there. Maybe they are and we can't see them." He glanced around again and started to feel like someone was watching them. It was just a gut feeling. But perhaps it was just because he *thought* he was being watched.

He peeked at Ashley, looked away then back again when he saw the intensity on her face as she stared into the darkness. "What is it?"

She rolled her lips inward. "I don't know, but I

thought I saw something over there."

"Like what?"

"Like someone lit a cigarette."

Jake immediately thought of the odd man he saw in the parking area. That could be a coincidence, of course, but it was sticking in his brain. It was just too much of a coincidence…so much in fact, that it was definitely *not* a coincidence.

Jake took a few serious steps off in the direction Ashley was looking but she grabbed his arm.

"No, Jake, don't."

"If someone's over there—"

"What? You're going to confront him with a snarky grin and get shot?"

"No, I'm—"

"You're not doing anything."

Jake looked down at Ariel but she was gone.

Chapter 16

Ariel

Ariel swam back home with more urgency than usual, ducking under the docks and swimming underwater for twenty seconds to get deep enough to enter her room. It was a long swim from Fort Fisher to her home up the river.

She popped up into the light of the room in which she'd spent her entire life. Her indoor pool was very much an outdoor lagoon. In the daytime, she had lots of natural light that fell through glass ceilings and walls with windows from nearly top-to-bottom. Natural rocks, smooth and comfortable, bordered the entire pool. Large automatic windows opened and closed to allow the ocean breezes to pass through.

She swam up and used the hanging rope to pull herself up onto her hammock bed from where, if she wanted, she could let her tail hang in the warm water. It needed to stay wet as often as possible, but it also didn't dry out that quickly. She'd never done it but she could probably go a day or two without being in water.

Just as she closed her eyes, she heard soft footsteps coming down the stone stairs that led up to the main house. She'd never been up there. Father was a doctor, as all the mermaid keepers had always been.

He turned the corner and smiled at her. "Ariel, my dear, how was your exercise this evening?"

"Fine."

"Have you eaten?"

She nodded. "I ate earlier." Her diet consisted of only vegetables, seeds, grains, fish and nuts.

"You've been taking longer than usual trips lately." He adjusted his small glasses and smoothed his white doctor's coat. He always wore his doctor's coat.

"I like the beaches at Fort Fisher."

He slowly closed his eyes. "Is that so?"

"Yes, they have big rocks that block me. It's also a lot darker, not as many lights. And people leave there earlier than the other beaches."

"Well, as long as you're careful."

"Of course, Father. I'm always careful."

He smiled. He had a kind smile and kind eyes when he smiled. "Of course you are, dear. You know I just worry about you."

"I know."

He turned to walk away.

"Father?"

He slowly turned. "Yes?"

"Why does it have to be like this?"

"Like what, dear?"

"Why do I have to die so young?"

He frowned. "Ariel," his voice firmed ever so slightly, "we've discussed this many times."

"I know, but lately, I've been more scared. I don't want to die."

"I don't want you to die, either. But there's nothing we can do about it. It's the cycle of life. When one is born, another must die."

"But why can I never know friendship? Why can I never know the camaraderie that your kind knows?"

"That's the way it has always been. The sea is yours."

"Why can I never know love?"

He sighed into a slouch that seemed to overcome his entire being. "I love you."

"Yes, I know. But you don't love me like people love each other. I see them. Young love, old love, and all the love in between. I see them on the beaches and in the boats. I see love everywhere. But I will never know that love."

"Ariel, don't do—"

"I want to fall in love," she interrupted.

He looked like tears were just micro measures away from coming. "I'm sorry, Ariel. I wish you could know it. I so very much wish. But it is what your kind has always done. I don't make the rules. I am only your guardian."

She rolled onto her back and looked up through the glass ceiling to the stars. "I just wish it could be different."

"I do too, my dear. I do too." He took a few steps toward the pool. "When your mother was your age, she went through the same things. It's natural to fear your own mortality. We humans do it too."

"But you get to enjoy so much more of it."

"I wish you could too. We enjoy life in many different ways. But you will know things that people will never know. You have lived a life that many people would love to live. You only see a small complexity of the human experience. There are many unpleasant aspects of it. Trust me when I tell you that many of them would change places with you."

"Yes, I know. But I feel like if I could love, then I could live with the hate and the cruelty that is your world. I want to experience everything life has to offer."

"And if there was any way possible for me to give those things to you I would."

She looked at him. "You're a doctor, can't you fix me? Why can't you save me? Why can't you make it so I can live to see my baby grow up? Why can't I live to feel love?"

He tilted his head. "All this talk of love suddenly. Why do you feel like this?"

She looked away. "I don't know. I guess it's just the way it is. I feel sadder now than ever before."

"Are you sure it's not something else? Is there something you want to tell me?"

"No."

"Are you sure?"

She shook her head. "I'm sure."

"Well, okay, my Ariel, but you can always tell me anything. Just like you always have."

"Please turn out my light."

He turned away from her, flipping the switch as he walked by.

In the darkness, the stars really shined. Ariel didn't fight her tears, she let them come. All she wanted was a friend. The loneliness was so hollow, it hurt so bad. The sadness never bothered her so much. She wasn't even sure what feeling this was inside. But it all of a sudden made her long to be touched, held, loved.

For weeks now, all she could think about was Jake. She didn't even know why. But ever since she'd seen him with a gun to his head, so sad, she hadn't stopped thinking about him. Her only happy moments of the day were when he was sitting on those rocks. Before she'd even spoken a word to him, he was on her mind.

Maybe it was because his sadness was even more profound than hers. Sadness was the one thing she'd always sensed in others. It was so easy for her to see it, maybe because she'd been living it for so long. Knowing sadness and loneliness so well didn't make them any easier to deal with. It just made them an all too familiar friend. Not a good friend, not the kind you call when you need something. But that friend that shows up when you really just want to be alone.

She longed for the days of her youth, when everything was fun and wonderful. She was never sad or lonely then. She loved her days and nights of frolicking in the ocean with not a care in the world. But now those days seemed so long ago. It was like those days were just wasted and lost forever.

Ariel reached across to the table near her bed and

grabbed her flashlight. She shined the powerful beam across the pool to where the pictures of the other mermaids hung on the wall. It saddened her that she never got to know her mother. It saddened her that her baby would never get to know her. Having accepted that this was just the way things were didn't make it easier. It bothered her that suddenly everything was bothering her. She wondered if she just swam away, if she wouldn't have a baby. She knew the tradition, she knew how it was supposed to work, but she didn't even care. She just wanted to be normal.

Chapter 17

Jake

Jake typed the keywords into the search engine. He hoped he'd be able to find something about Bruce Shepard. He wasn't filled with high hopes, since it was probably a common name.

As suspected, the Internet was mostly unhelpful. There was nothing on a local Bruce Shepard whatsoever. He must have remembered the name incorrectly or something. But he was usually good with that stuff. He tried a bunch of alternate spellings. There was nothing.

"Anything?" Ashley asked as she sat down next to him.

"Negative."

"Did you try different spellings?"

"Sort of," he lied.

"Did you try just searching Shepard, with one P and two Ps?"

Just searching the last name, the double-P version retrieved no results, but the single-P search did bring up a Belden Shepard in Wilmington. "There's a Belden Shepard, one P, listed off of River Road. He's a doctor, out of a small office called Intercoastal Medical Associates."

"Maybe that's your guy."

"Maybe." He did some more searching and came up with another thing. There was an article mentioning a Bruce Shepard, a doctor. "Here's something interesting, there's a Bruce Shepard listed in this article on local businesses, he's also a doctor.

"Gotta be the same guy."

"Maybe Bruce is Belden."

"Let's drive by the house."

Jake nodded and grabbed his keys.

* * *

They pulled up to the private gated community and drove down to the house. It wasn't right on the water, but the property had a small inlet river that led right along the rear of the structure. There were only three other houses down this private road and they were all equally large.

Ashley eyed the house. "That could definitely be a doctor's house."

"It's someone who has money, that's for sure."

"That's a lot of house." She leaned back. "What's that big thing in the back? Is that all glass?"

He nodded. "It must be a greenhouse or pool or something."

"Must be a pool, why would you tint a

greenhouse?"

"True."

"That's a big pool."

"Huge." He stopped the car. "Should we knock?"

Ashley made a face at him. "And say what? Excuse me, sir, can we see your mermaid?"

"I hadn't thought about it."

"Well, you better come up with something if you plan on knocking on the guy's door."

Jake sighed and started to drive slowly past the house.

"You're giving up?" Ashley asked.

"I don't know what else to do."

"Stop the car."

"Why?"

"I don't give up that easily. I have an idea."

Ashley got out and started toward the white iron fence that surrounded the house. Jake turned off the car and followed. They came up to the gate at the sidewalk. Ashley tried to open it but it was locked. There was an intercom on a pole. She thumbed the button.

"What are you going to say?"

"Sshh...don't worry."

They waited a long time but there was no answer. Jake was about to turn back about ten times but Ashley was persistent and refused to give up. She rang the bell again, and again, and again.

"I don't think anyone is going to answer."

"Maybe not, but I'm giving them every chance to get pissed off enough to do something stupid."

"You have a knack for making people do stupid things."

"It's my gift."

After another minute, even Ashley was about to give up, but the speaker box cracked and a man said, "How can I help you?"

"Is this Dr. Shepard?"

"Who's calling?"

Ashley turned a devious smile. "My name is Jessica Finch. I'm here from the UNCW Marine Biology special studies team. We wanted to ask you a few questions about a research paper."

There was a long pause until he replied, "I think you have the wrong house."

"I'm looking for Dr. Shepard."

"I don't see how I can help you. Good day."

"Wait, sir? Sir, it will only take a moment of your time. Please, sir?" Ashley pleaded but there was no response. Finally, she turned away and headed back to the car.

Jake shut his door and turned the key. "Guess that didn't go over well."

"Not so much."

He spun the car around and headed back down the street. As they drove slowly past an older woman at her mailbox, giving them the evil eye, Ashley said, "Stop, I want to talk to her."

Jake slowed the car until Ashley's window was next to the woman. "Hi."

The old woman's wrinkled face scrunched up even more. Facial tics carried from her cheeks to her lips. "You're not welcome there."

"Huh?" Ashley replied.

The old woman thrust her bony-elbowed arm up and pointed at the Shepard house. "There. You're not welcome there."

"No, we weren't."

"No one's welcome there. No one's ever been welcome there."

"Why's that?"

She waved her hand. "Who knows? I've lived here twenty-eight years and that bastard has never spoken a word to me. 'Who in the hell, I wonder,' I said, 'who lives across the street from someone for nearly three decades and never says a word to them?'"

"I don't know."

"No one, that's who. No one! He's a horrible little man, a sniveling weakling, and he's not a very good doctor, either."

"No?"

"Hell no. My sister went to see him once and he flubbed her care terribly. He said she had a cold and she had pneumonia so bad she nearly died. It was a catastrophe. I swear he's incompetent."

"Sorry to hear."

"They should've pulled his license by now. I can't believe he has any patients left the way he treats people. He's not even...I think he's a snake oil salesman. He prescribed my sister the wrong...he never washes his house. It just looks dirty all the time. And one time he got my mail by mistake and he just threw it out. I know it was him. I just know it was. I was waiting for that check for weeks. I had to call the Social Security office, and I was on hold for two hours, and he threw it away." She pointed to the house again. "What'd you want over there, anyway?"

"Umm, we're part of a UNCW research team, and someone told us he has some...marine life in captivity."

The old woman narrowed her eyes. "Wouldn't surprise me. He's probably got all kinds of stuff going on in there. He's always up all hours of the night." She moved closer to the car. "You should talk to his old partner. I bet he could tell you some stories."

"Who's that?"

"Roger Pender. He was a great doctor but Shepard pushed him out, made him retire early."

"How come?"

"Meh, who the heck knows what went on, but Roger probably should have sued him, I bet."

Without another word, the old woman turned away and headed up her sidewalk.

Jake slowly pulled away. "What do you make of that?"

Ashley leaned back into her seat. "Clearly she's delusional."

"That's obvious."

"But she did say something that made me think that maybe he's hiding something."

"Well, I think we know what he's hiding."

"Yeah."

"What we need to know is who the heck he really is and if the wild gunman is his."

Ashley brought her hand to her face to wipe away the tears that started coming.

"Ashley, I'm sorry."

She laughed. "This is stupid. I shouldn't even be sad. I hated him."

"You didn't hate him."

"No, I really had grown to hate him."

"But you loved him at one time."

She nodded. "Yeah. I mean, I think I did. Sometimes I wonder if I even know what love really is. You know?"

Jake shrugged.

Ashley touched his arm. "Hey, that's just me. I don't doubt you loved Cassie."

"That's the reality of it. Love is a twisted game. It's ephemeral, it's not forever no matter how hard we try. Unless both people want it to last forever, and the Universe wants it to last forever. You've suffered a loss. Even if you stopped loving him a while ago, that loss is going to hurt."

"Is that when it hit you?"

He pulled to a stop at the end of the rural road intersection. "I loved Cassie, but I had my doubts about marriage. I think everyone does."

Ashley nodded. "She loved you a lot. She loved everyone."

"She loved hard. She used to say that all the time."

"I guess we all should. We should all wear our heart on our sleeve like Cassie did. It made people want to be near her, it made her the center of every gathering."

Jake pursed his lips. "I guess that was part of the reason it hurt so much to lose her. I didn't just lose her, I lost everything. All my friends were her friends. All my hobbies were her hobbies. We shared a life and when she was gone, it felt like everything was gone."

"I know—I saw it happening. When you stopped hanging with your friends for her. I knew it wasn't going to be good for your soul."

"Other than my bike shop, everything was all about her. She and my friends, they didn't really jive. It wasn't so much that I wanted to stop hanging out with them, or she asked me to. It was just I wanted to be with her all the time."

"That's what love does. I only know because the same thing happened with Mike. I stopped hanging out with all my friends, but it was because he didn't like them. He didn't like anyone that was in my life before we were married. He wanted me to be all his. At first I was flattered, but later it seemed like a way of controlling me."

"Of course it was."

"I was stupid and in love. Or what I thought was love."

Jake shook his head. "Love makes everyone stupid...even if it's not quite real or not quite right."

Ashley sighed. "Make no mistake. Love is a drug. It's every bit as addicting, confusing, dangerous, and beautiful as any drug on this planet. Love gives you the ability to both move mountains and lose everything in the next moment. It's a struggle for survival against something we can't control. Yet we judge each other for making the same mistakes we ourselves have either made before or are guaranteed to make at some point."

"Geez, when you put it like that it makes love seem like an evil monster."

"It is, Jake. Love is an evil monster. But at the same time it's the most beautiful and amazing thing on Earth. And that's why we keep chasing the demon. We're willing to plow through terrible relationships and experiences in hopes that that one amazing love is out there waiting for us. It's hardwired into our DNA. We want that feeling; we crave that high."

When a car behind them blared its horn, Jake realized they were still sitting at the intersection. He met her eyes briefly, and then checked the traffic before pulling out onto the main road. "I want to find Roger Pender."

Ashley nodded. "Me too."

Chapter 18

Castro

Castro picked up his phone and waited for the call to connect. "It's me. The scare tactics didn't work. He's still seeing her."

"Scare tactics? Scare tactics! Is that what you call it?"

"It was collateral damage."

"You do realize your mistake took an innocent man?"

"That was unfortunate. I had to defend myself."

"I thought you were some kind of professional?"

Castro chewed the inside of his lip and took a deep breath. "I do what I have to."

The man on the other end of the phone grunted in frustration. "Fine, what's done is done. But it's time we up the stakes."

"I need a little time."

"Why?"

"There can't be another body so soon."

"That's not a viable excuse. Get it done."

"Then I need a boat, a big one that can go deep." If he was going to kill two more people he needed to be sure no bodies were found for a long time after he was out of town. He had a job to do down in Miami when this one was over. If he had a boat, he could drop the bodies out in the Atlantic a hundred miles away from here. Either that or he needed to find an alternative.

"I will get you a boat. Just tell me when and where and I'll have it ready. I just need you to eliminate the problems before they get too big."

"It's your nickel."

"Good, get it done. We can't take another chance. Go with the plan for tonight, the one we talked about. I've made some other arrangements to cover things."

"It's risky."

"Just do it, don't alter the plan now."

"And if he does?"

"We'll deal with that bridge when we need to cross it."

Castro ended the call. He hated the idea of someone else pushing him into a move he didn't approve of. But they were insistent and offered to double his pay. For that, he would take a few more risks.

* * *

Ariel

Ariel woke up earlier than usual and leveraged herself so the sun fell on her face. Arms stretched above her head, she enjoyed the warmth with a purposeful yawn.

For half the night, she tossed and turned. Her mind churned with questions. What Jake had said about Father watching her seemed impossible. At first. But the more she thought about it, the more she started to wonder.

How could he be watching her? There was no way he could. She never told him where she was going, she never told anyone. He certainly didn't swim like she did. No one could. She'd spent her life in the water, and although she couldn't keep up with the dolphins and belugas, she could hold pace with them for a bit at their cruising speeds.

With a sigh, she slid into the water and caught a deep breath before swimming down to the bottom of her pool. By pure instinct, she went toward the tunnel to the intercoastal river waters that would lead her out to the sea.

In less than twenty seconds, she was popping up into the garden area where no prying eyes would ever see her. Lush vegetation grew tall on all sides and thick trees hanged over her head, only allowing daggers of sunlight to dance on the lagoon.

She swam over to the greenhouse and plucked a fresh orange from the tree. While peeling and eating her orange, her usual day planning started to unfold. On most days, she'd go for a long swim, then search for some shells to add to her collection, then come back and read. She loved to read, it was her favorite thing to do. The people in her books had such fantastical adventures. Letting them take her away to their world was so much fun it made her forget for a while who she was…*what* she was.

Never before in her life had she wished so hard to be someone else. She just wanted to be human. She wanted to be a girl like Ashley, who could walk around and hold hands with Jake.

Sitting on the rocks, she reached down and punched her tail. "Stupid fin, I hate you!" She picked up a broken seashell and started scoring the skin of her tail until it left a mark.

The skin didn't have any feeling, she'd always hated that part. Father would get mad when she would cut her tail on something because he would have to perform a fix. He said because she couldn't feel anything infection could set in and get very bad.

Right now, she didn't care. She used the seashell to score the thick skin, digging at it deeper and deeper. Part of her wanted to just keep going until it did hurt, like the time she got hit by the boat when she was twelve. She'd accidentally surfaced in front of a boat, it hit her, and cut her tail all the way to the blood. Father had to perform surgery. It wasn't the first time she'd hurt herself, nor the last, but it was the worst.

She headed out of the waterway until she got to the clearing of the ocean. Diving into the waves, she swam as hard and fast as possible for several minutes and finally surfaced way out past the breakers. Swimming north, she kept going until she reached one of the most populated beaches in the area, Carolina Beach.

Just sitting there, bobbing in the water, looking back at the shore, she never wanted to just swim over and slide up onto the sand more than she did right now. A couple times, she'd let people glimpse her, just to see what they would do. Usually she'd pick a little girl, and then watch her run to her family and tell them what she'd seen. Maybe that was mean in a way, because the families never believed. They used to just smile and pat the girls on the head or marvel at their imaginations with wide-mouthed smiles. A couple times, she'd gotten too close to the lifeguard towers and caused them to become worried when she popped up and went back under. But she usually stayed far enough out and the fin would always just leave them thinking they'd probably seen a dolphin.

She didn't see any families hanging around this side of the beach. Tourist season was going to end soon and people were already heading back up to the cold north. Ariel had never seen snow but she wanted to badly. One of her favorite books was *Call of the Wild* by Jack London. It was a wonderful adventure.

After a few more moments in the waves, she decided to head back home. It was going to get busy out here soon and she wasn't allowed to be in the waters when it was busy.

The swim went by quickly. She didn't see any of her dolphin friends, which told her maybe the weather was going to get bad later. There were some darker clouds rolling into the area.

She popped up in her pool and saw Father standing at the edge.

"I was expecting you sooner," he said.

She blinked away the water from her eyes.

"Sorry, I was just enjoying the view."

He squatted down. "Ariel, it's time."

"Time for what?"

The look on his face said it all. "It's time."

She didn't want to believe it. She didn't want to accept it. In a few months, she would give birth and die.

Chapter 19

Jake

The retirement community, a sprawling campus, was unlike anything Jake pictured in his head when those words conjured images. It reminded him of a college that started out small and kept adding on. None of the buildings matched perfectly, they all had a similar color and shape, but they were just different enough to tell they were built at different times and probably by different people. The place was nice, the large grassy areas were well-groomed and the water features looked so clean they were making him thirsty. The nearby crashing ocean waves just over the bluff were soft but constant.

"There." Ashley pointed. "That building, that's the Sea Pine."

Jake eyed the tan and white building.

They walked up to the structure where a middle-aged woman in a powder blue button-down shirt and khaki shorts smiled while she stood behind a small table. "Welcome to Sea Pine at Holiday

Sands."

Ashley extended her hand. "Hi, I'm Ashley, this is Jake. We're looking for Roger Pender. We were told by the office he lived in this building."

The woman nodded. "Roger is in the courtyard right now around back. We're welcoming a new resident today." She motioned with her hand. "We throw a little party to welcome them, so just follow the smell of barbeque. You're welcome to grab a bite to eat."

Ashley smiled. "Thank you so much."

They headed around the building where a gathering of people milled about. Most of the people were seniors, but there were a few kids roaming with other younger adults. Jake had to assume they were friends or relatives, since as far as he knew, this place was only for retired people. He'd never been to this place, but he knew from people around that it was one of the most expensive retirement communities on all of the Carolina coast. It was definitely less retirement community and more luxury resort. They had their own private beach access, a golf course, four swimming pools—two of which were indoors—a huge fitness facility, a gourmet restaurant, and a shopping center with grocery store. One could live here and almost never leave the campus. The more Jake looked around, the more he wanted to live here right now.

Ashley walked up to an older woman with soft blue eyes. "Hi, we're looking for Roger Pender."

The woman had a slight tremor in her hand, but seemed otherwise healthy. "That's Roger over there." She pointed to a tall, muscular man with a full head of salt-and-pepper hair, round glasses and a strong jaw. He stood there looking out at the ocean.

Ashley approached him. "Mr. Pender?"

He glanced at her but looked back at the water. "Who's asking?"

"My name is Ashley and this is Jake."

"Are you celebrities?"

Ashley made a face and shrugged. "No."

"Then you must have last names."

"This is Jake Wheeler, and I'm Ashley Robertson."

Roger sipped his glass of red wine. "What can I help you with, Miss Robertson?"

"We wanted to speak with you about your old business partner, Bruce Shepard."

Roger smirked and started to walk away. "This conversation is over."

Ashley chased after him. "Please, sir, this is an important matter. It's a matter of life and death."

He turned and gave her an odd look. Then he looked over at Jake. "It often is with Shepard. He's a terrible doctor. But I'm not getting involved in any malpractice lawsuit. Sorry." He walked on.

"Wait, please." Ashley hurried into his path. "This is not about malpractice or a lawsuit of any kind."

Roger narrowed his eyes, moving them back and forth between her and Jake. "What *is* this about?"

"We just want to know about Dr. Shepard."

"Why?"

Jake offered, "Curiosity?"

Roger laughed. "I don't think so. People don't

track down a loosely associated former colleague because of simple curiosity."

Jake started to mutter a wise remark but Ashley gave him a look that said, *Let me do the talking.* Jake knew how persuasive Ashley could be so he didn't want to argue with her point.

She looked back at Roger. "Look, Mr. Pender, I know this is weird and probably out of the blue, but someone close to me was just murdered, and we think it has something to do with Dr. Shepard."

"Murdered?" He turned to face her more directly. "How?"

"He was shot."

Roger looked to the sea. "You're talking about the man who was shot on the island?"

Ashley nodded. "Yes."

"The realtor, Mike Robertson, he was related to you?"

"He was my husband."

Roger turned his head. "I'm sorry for your loss. I never had the opportunity to work with him, but I'm told he was a fine realtor and a good man."

"Thank you."

"But how, may I ask, is this related to Dr. Shepard?"

"We think the man who killed Mike was trying," she pointed to Jake, "to kill him."

"That doesn't answer my question."

Jake offered, "It's complicated."

Roger looked at Ashley. "Explain it to me."

Ashley sighed. "We think that Dr. Shepard hired this man."

Roger laughed. "Why would Shepard hire

someone to kill you?"

Jake shrugged. "He doesn't like me."

He stared at Jake an uncomfortable amount of time. "I'm sure a lot of people don't like you. It doesn't mean they want to kill you."

Ashley lied, "Jake is a key witness in a malpractice suit against the doctor."

Roger looked away and emptied his wine glass. It wasn't empty for more than five seconds before a man in a white uniform approached him with a bottle and offered to top off the glass, which he accepted. The man then slid away to the next guest.

Roger sipped more wine. "So you lied to my face."

"Umm…oh…" Ashley replied.

Roger pressed on. "Doctors face those kinds of lawsuits all the time. It's no reason to kill anyone. I can't help you. You've come to the wrong place."

"Please, Dr. Pender," Ashley pleaded. "I can feel in my heart that this man—"

"No, don't! You're barking up the wrong tree. Belden is no killer."

"But—"

"No but, no nothing."

Jake jumped in. "So you're just going to let him kill me? You're a pathetic excuse for a man."

Roger stepped closer to Jake. "You'd better watch your mouth, son. I may be twice your age, but I spend six days a week at the gym. I will not hesitate to knock your block off."

Jake sneered at him. "Go right ahead, old man. I'm not afraid of you. I'm not afraid of anything. I sat on the rocks at Fort Fisher for a month with a pistol to my head, itching to pull the trigger, looking for the courage."

"My point exactly. If you had any balls, you'd have pulled that trigger."

"I was about to, until something—someone—very extraordinary appeared to me from the sea." Roger's face went slack and Jake could tell right away that he knew. "I think Shepard has a little secret. And his little secret is going to get me killed."

Roger ran his fingers under his glasses and rubbed his eyes. He then slowly started to walk toward the shore. "Belden has always been eccentric, a little strange even. I didn't want to go into business with him, but he was fresh out of med school and had a bank account busting with cash. I'd been in practice for just a few years and was struggling to pay the rent. Here comes this hotshot tossing around big numbers, an advertising budget so big he wanted to spend more in a week than I spent all year."

"So you did what you had to do."

Roger narrowed his gaze. "I did what I felt was best. I'm a doctor, and I wanted to help as many people as possible. It was never about the money for me. But I couldn't reach anyone with my practice. When Belden came on, business went up tenfold."

"That's all well and good."

"It was to me."

"So you've been to his house?"

Roger stopped at the crest of the hill overlooking the sea just about ten feet below. "I have."

"You've seen her."

He met Jake's eyes, almost gauging how to respond. After a long moment, he seemingly gave up trying to hide anything. "She was hurt. At first, he resisted my help, but I forced my way into the scene. But he still wouldn't let me assist on the operation at first. But there was some vascular bleeding in the upper thigh area that he struggled with. I was able to stop the bleeding and get things sorted out."

"But you didn't see what she was?"

"Not at first, not until after. But what was I going to do? He made valid points about her becoming a freak show. She was just a little kid, so I forced myself to forget. And I hadn't spoken of it in over ten years until this moment."

"How didn't you know while you were assisting?"

"She was covered except for the wound. And frankly, there was nothing different that I noticed. Internally she looked just like you or I would."

"And when you saw it, your curiosity didn't drive you crazy?"

Roger shrugged. "I stayed busy with my work. I didn't have time to dissect it, and after a few weeks it was more or less out of my mind. It's like seeing a UFO, you don't want believe it, so it's easy to forget it."

"He never mentioned it again?"

"Not a word. But I could feel him thinking it sometimes. He wondered if I was going to keep the secret."

"How come he didn't try to kill you?"

Roger looked at him and shrugged. "Like I said,

Belden is not a killer. And even if he was, he knows I'm not a threat. I'm not about to turn that girl, whatever she is, into some sort of freak. She doesn't threaten my existence."

"I'm not about to, either. So what makes me different?"

"I can't tell you that."

Ashley asked, "How come it's so hard to find information on Dr. Bruce Shepard?"

Roger looked at her. "I wasn't aware it was."

"There's almost nothing on him. We looked up Bruce Shepard, but everything goes to some old country singer from the seventies."

"Bruce is not his real name, it's a nickname. Did you try Albert Belden Shepard, or A. Belden Shepard?"

"No."

"His medical license is under Albert Belden Shepard."

"That would explain a lot," Ashley replied.

Roger turned away from the view. "I've told you all I could."

"Are you sure? Because I don't trust this psychopath won't still kill us," Jake asked.

Roger cast a knowing smile. "Belden is the furthest thing from a psychopath. He's not even a sociopath."

"What's the difference?" Jake asked flippantly.

"The difference is that if you know what to look for, you can always spot a sociopath, they're narcissistic and egocentric. They are masters of manipulation. You can't always spot a psychopath, and by the time you do, it's too late. Now, if you'll excuse me, I have a prior commitment." He turned away and headed back toward the building.

Ashley stood next to Jake and asked, "Do you think he's telling us everything?"

Jake shook his head. "Not a chance. He's too smart to tell us anything."

"Why did he tell us what he did?"

"Why indeed."

Chapter 20

Jake looked across the ratty old table at Ashley. Her long hair was draped over her left shoulder. She stroked it while she silently read off the laptop screen, moving her lips ever so slightly. He could not look away.

"What?" she asked, startling him.

"What?"

"I don't know. It looked like you wanted to say something."

He shook his head. "No."

She sighed. "It's already ten? Geez, it feels like we've been doing this for hours."

"We *have* been doing this for hours."

She leaned back. "There's nothing here. There's nothing that's going to tell us anything."

"Doesn't seem that way."

"Where's Tom?"

"He's off to Florida for the month."

"Wow, the whole month? For what?"

"Some deep sea fishing thing he does every year."

"What, there's no deep sea fishing off the coast of the Carolinas?" Sarcasm dripped off her words.

"I guess he's going to fish for something that's not as popular up here. I don't know. I don't fish."

"But you love eating fish, isn't that ironic?"

"I like any food I don't have to work for."

"Lazy modern American."

He playfully tossed a balled up napkin at her. "Says you."

She threw it back with impressive velocity. It whizzed past his head and bounced off the old wooden cabinets. "Careful, you might break the house."

"It is in a woeful state."

"The rent is cheap."

"It better be."

"Cheapest I've found."

"It should be free."

"You're just saying that because of the palmetto bugs."

"I think those are cockroaches."

"I think they're the same thing."

Ashley got up and walked to the fridge to grab the wine. "What happened with your house?"

He stretched his arms above his head. "It's still for sale."

"Why don't you just keep it?"

He shrugged. "I guess I'm afraid I won't be able to get Cassie's memory out of it."

"But she never lived in it."

"I know, but we bought it together. She picked it out. It was her baby. I don't know, I guess it just felt weird to stay there."

"That's fair."

"Would you stay in your house now?"

She looked to the ceiling and pursed her lips. "No, I guess I wouldn't."

Jake stretched his shoulders. "How're you doing, by the way?"

"I don't know. It's weird."

"I guess that's one way to put it."

"I mean, I don't know how to feel. Or, maybe I don't know what I'm feeling."

"Aren't you sad? You've known Mike for a long time."

"Eleven years."

"That's a long time."

She took a long swig of wine. "I'm not as sad as I should be."

"And you feel guilty about that."

She looked up from her hands and met his eyes. "I'm a horrible person."

"No—no, you're not. I understand exactly what you mean. As time has gone on, I've felt less sad over Cassie and Paul. But I didn't want to."

"Time heals all wounds."

"I guess. But I didn't want it to. I wanted to hold onto that pain. I started to crave it, it became me, consumed me. And I felt that if I let it go, then I was letting her go. I mean, I've said this ten times to myself, maybe in an effort to understand it."

Ashley reached across the small table and squeezed his hand. "It's okay to let her go. It doesn't mean you loved her any less. And it doesn't mean you'll forget her."

Jake bit back his emotions and looked down at

Ashley's delicate hands. He had a plethora of words in his head, but couldn't get any of them out, not the ones he really wanted to. So he settled for the easiest ones. "Thanks, Ashley. I don't know what I would've done without you these last few days. I'm really sorry I got you so wrapped up in this."

"Jake, this is some crazy shit." She leaned forward and crossed her arms on the table. "There's a fricken mermaid swimming off the coast of North Carolina. Do you know how insane that is?" She chuffed. "Of course you do, what am I saying?"

"And you thought I was crazy."

"Of course I did."

"Don't worry, so did I."

Ashley made a face and stuck her nose in the air, sniffing hard. "Do you smell that?"

Jake mimicked her. "I don't smell anything."

"I have a very good nose."

"What do you smell?"

"Gas."

"Gas, as in gasoline, or propane?"

"Gasoline."

Jake sniffed again. He didn't smell it at first, but then he did get a slight whiff of it. But it was nothing more than what might have dripped out of a lawnmower or something. "I can barely smell it."

Ashley got up. "Trust me, I can smell it."

Jake followed her to the front door of the small bungalow and peered outside. "Maybe my car sprang a leak. It is old and things are breaking all the time."

Ashley moved away from the front of the house and down the hallway toward the backyard. "I think

158

it's coming from the back of the house."

Jake kept looking out front at his car, but didn't see anything. He did smell gas though now, more than he did a second ago. Of course, maybe that was just in his head because Ashley had talked about it. Maybe it wasn't getting any worse at all.

"Whoa!" Ashley exclaimed from the back bedroom.

He hurried toward her. "What?" But after the word came out of his mouth, he smelled it too. "Oh!"

"We gotta get out of here." She turned quickly and bumped into him.

The explosion hammered at her back and tore into the side of the house.

The concussion of the blast threw Ashley into Jake with impressive force and they both fell in the hallway. Roiling flames painted the ceiling above them, reaching out for fuel to latch onto like busy fingers.

Jake helped push Ashley to her feet with a well-placed hand to her ass, and then sprang up and headed toward the front door. She twisted the handle and pushed, but the door didn't open. Jake shoved her out of the way and slammed into it with everything he had, but it didn't budge. The top part pulled away from the frame but it didn't move at the bottom. Then with another whoosh of scorching heat and fire, flames consumed the front of the house in earnest.

Looking to his right, he saw the kitchen windows were still clear. He ran and grabbed Ashley's hand, dragging her through the kitchen. In one motion, he wrapped his arms around her and jumped back-first through the tall glass, landing hard on his back onto the deteriorated concrete sidewalk.

Between his weight, Ashley's weight, and the hard ground, Jake felt every ounce of breath blast from his body. Ashley rolled off him and sprang to her feet. Jake struggled a few seconds on the ground, trying to get air into his lungs.

Ashley reached down and pulled him up as she scurried away from the house while another explosion ruptured the side of the structure, sending a column of fire and smoke into the night sky.

They got to the street and turned back to face the inferno as sirens bellowed in the distance.

After catching his breath, Jake hurried out the words, "Too close."

Ashley bent to put her hands on her knees. "That's the understatement of the year."

Fire trucks turned the corner as Jake watched all his belongings burn.

Chapter 21

Castro

Castro answered his phone and needed more effort than usual to utter, "Yeah."

"Is it done?"

He didn't even want to answer. He'd missed the mark yet again. He'd never in his career had such a hard time with a job. He considered himself a superior killing machine. His work was usually spotless and untraceable…and it was untraceable because it was spotless. But he listened to them and changed his plan, and the results were less than perfect. He cleared his throat twice, took a long pause before he answered. "Not done."

"What?" The anger over the phone was palpable. "I've paid you a ton of money to do your job."

"I know what you've paid me for."

"I don't think you do, because so far you've accidentally killed an innocent man, and missed the mark twice."

"Hey, we're on the phone."

"I don't care. You're screwing up and I don't have time for this."

"I've missed the mark once. The first time was an unforeseen complication."

"It's still an excuse for incompetence. I don't like complications."

"Neither do I, but sometimes they cannot be avoided. The world is an imperfect place."

There was a long grunt. "Now what? How are you going rectify the situation?"

Castro fixed the collar of his ugly Hawaiian shirt. "Don't worry."

"I am worried. You've not exactly instilled me with confidence. Do I have to find someone else?"

Castro cleared his throat. "That will bring more complications. When you start contacting multiple people that do what I do, you increase the chances that someone out there will talk. If someone talks, you're going to be unhappy, very—very unhappy with the results."

There was a long pause on the other end of the phone. "Fine. Just get it done and make sure it—"

"I know what to do."

"Then do it." He hung up the phone.

Castro lit his cigarette and took a long drag. It did bother him that the last detonator didn't ignite. The house was supposed to have been engulfed in flames long before those two were able to jump through that glass. The only explanation was that the pop detonator was defective. It wasn't the first time one didn't light. Fire was not his preferred means as a killing agent. He didn't mind using it as cleaning agent. Even so, usually the marks were caught enough by surprise that it didn't matter. He had to hand it to those two; they were quick thinkers. But more than that, they were lucky, and their luck was going to run out. Everyone's did.

* * *

Jake

Jake kicked at some of the burnt ashes left from his latest personal disaster. The fire department had just rolled away. The police had asked all the pertinent questions, what happened next was out of his hands. They knew it was arson, but knowing and doing anything about it were two different things. The police force on the island was small, and unless this turned into a serial case, chances are they weren't going to get much more help than the county sheriffs.

Ashley gave him an unexpected, hard hug, which forced an, "Oh!" to escape him.

"I'm sorry, Jake."

"It's not your fault."

"No, but I'm still sorry."

"At least my car survived."

She eased her way out of the hug. "Yeah, but they sprayed so much water on it I wonder if it will ever run again."

Jake went over to the old Volkswagen and opened the door. When he twisted the key he didn't expect it to start, but it did. After a few coughs and sputters, the old horse was running perfect. "Hey, she's a runner."

Ashley got in. "Good, let's get out of here. I can't stand this smell anymore."

They headed down the road. Jake started laughing.

Ashley looked at him oddly. "What's so funny?"

"We're both homeless. We both technically own houses and we're homeless."

"That's not funny." Then Ashley joined in on his laughter. "Okay, it's kinda funny." She ended her tired laugh and said, "Mine is still a crime scene."

Jake's laughter sucked away. "When can you go back in?"

"I don't know. But I don't want to go back. I'm just going to put it on the market and get rid of it. I'm sure Leo will sell it for me. He'll probably take over all of Mike's clients. He'll be ecstatic to sell it. It's probably worth twice what we paid for it."

Jake sighed. "I guess we could go to my house...but it's empty. There's no place to sleep and I don't have a key."

Ashley laughed again, longer than she should have. It turned into an uncontrollable laugh. It was so infectious that Jake started to laugh for no reason other than the fact she was laughing.

With laughter-drenched words, Jake managed, "Why're we laughing?"

She replied, barely able to get the words out, "I—don't—know."

Finally after the hysteria wound down, Jake said, "Let's just get a hotel for tonight. I can't think anymore."

She let out a long raspy groan. "Agreed."

As they headed past the huge oceanfront

Marriott, Ashley pointed. "There, let's stay there."

"That place is out of my budget."

"It's on me. I think we deserve it."

They checked in, and had another good laugh when the clerk at the desk asked them if they had luggage. They didn't want to get into it, but he looked like he wanted an explanation. He didn't get one.

They headed through the spacious lobby to the elevators, and up to the eighth floor room. After walking through the suite doors, Ashley immediately stepped out onto the balcony that overlooked the ocean. "Wow, this is amazing. No matter how many times I've seen this view, it's still amazing."

"How many times have you been up here?"

"Several times. When I was doing real estate, I used to bring the high end clients up here and pay for them to stay a night while they were thinking things over."

"Why did you give up the real estate game? You were really good at it."

"Too good."

"I don't get it."

"Well, Mike didn't like me showing him up. His fragile male ego couldn't handle it."

"Is that why he went out on his own?"

"Initially yes. But it still didn't help because then we were competing for clients."

"But you were married. What did it matter?"

"My argument exactly. But he was always my money and his money, it was never our money."

"That's neurotic."

"Well, needless to say, I decided it was best to step away and just find something else to do. I had my broker's license, so I started teaching other agents and eventually the real estate consulting business was born. I didn't have to compete against Mike, but I could still stay in the game to some extent."

Jake stepped to her, leaning on the railing. "The sunrise is going to be spectacular from up here."

"I imagine. Just look at the sky."

A nearly full moon swayed over the ocean like one of those old garage light bulbs that hung from the ceiling. A shimmering white glow seemed to spill out from the dark all the way to the sand below. "It's amazing."

He looked at her. The moonlight on her face made her look even more beautiful than she already was. She must have felt him staring, because she met his eyes.

He blew a breath. "I'm trying really hard not to kiss you right now."

"I feel like we've been here before."

"Different time, different place, same dilemma."

"There was a good reason not to kiss me last time."

"Two good reasons."

"There isn't one now." She reached up and put her hand on his cheek. "There won't ever be one again."

Jake could feel his heart clacking like a diesel engine. He didn't want to resist her perfectly curved lips. He'd had countless dreams of kissing Ashley, dreams that felt so real he'd wake up thinking it had

166

happened, dreams where he chose Ashley over Cassie when given the opportunity, dreams he didn't want to be dreams, but they always were. They were dreams, until now.

He leaned in and tasted her for the first time. Years of anticipation culminated into the most amazing kiss he'd ever experienced. Every part of him started to tremble until he sank deeper into the kiss and let go. The vibrations that ran through his body settled into something both exciting and natural. He wanted to make love to her right on that balcony. His hands fished up her shirt, feeling the curve of her back, the tightness of her waist. He wanted to feel all of her, but he pulled his lips away and just hugged her tightly.

She wrapped her arms around his neck and squeezed. "My God, Jake," she whispered. "Why did we wait so long to do that?"

"I guess the best things take time." He didn't want her to let go. He just wanted to stay embraced forever. It just felt so right to have her in his arms. Their bodies just seemed to fit together so perfectly. It was like they were once part of the same mold that had been broken apart and the two pieces finally reunited.

It seemed like the hug went on forever until Ashley finally slid away from him. "I really need to shower."

"Me too, I smell like fire." As he watched her walk toward the bathroom, he never wanted anyone more in his life. Her body just looked so perfect. But this was not the time for such things. He would not even try. Still, part of him wished she'd offer for him to join her in the shower. After about three minutes of the water running, however, he knew that wasn't going to happen and the moment of passion had siphoned away from his body and mind.

With nothing to occupy his thoughts, he took out his phone and started reading some of the pages they'd found on Dr. Shepard. It seemed like an exercise in futility. They'd combed over hundreds of pages between the two of them and nothing really stood out. The doctor was up to something, there was no doubt in his mind. What could be proven, on the other hand, was another thing entirely.

The words on the page seemed to blend into a giant block of babble. Then the link to an article intrigued him so he followed it, mostly because it was a different color than the rest of the text.

It seemed that Dr. Shepard had taken part in an experimental procedure to help a young boy who had been badly burned in a chemical accident. The article went on to talk about an experimental skin grafting procedure. At first, this didn't really mean anything to him, but then something about it made his skin crawl.

Ashley must have read something on his face, because when she stepped out of the bathroom, she asked, "What's wrong?"

Jake looked up, taking in her toweled form. "Maybe nothing…probably maybe."

"Looks like something."

"Well, it might be nothing, but it might be something."

"You're talking like a broken moron. Lay it on me, Sherlock."

"Dr. Shepard assisted in an experimental skin grafting operation. They were trying to save a little boy who'd been burned."

"Did it work?"

"Huh?"

"Did the kid make it? Did it work?"

He scanned the article. "No, it says the procedure was somewhat successful but the patient passed away due to complications of the procedure."

She toweled her hair. "What else does it say?"

He shrugged. "Not much."

"And you think this is significant because…?" She dragged out the word.

Jake threw his hands up. "I don't know. But maybe Ariel's existence has another explanation besides supernatural."

She laughed uncomfortably. "What, you think he grafted some dolphin skin onto a little girl?"

Jake winced at both the absurdity of that concept, and the fact that it felt less absurd than the reality of an actual mermaid existing. "I don't know. I guess that's as stupid as a mermaid really existing."

Ashley issued a mock whistling noise. "Jake, you've gone around the bend, I think."

He stood. "Have I really?" He started to pace. "I mean, think about this. What's more likely, that some crazy Dr. Frankenstein mutilated some little girl for the sake of medicine, or there really is a supernatural creature roaming the waters off the coast of North Carolina?"

Ashley shrugged. "What do you want me to say

here?"

"I want you to say what you think."

"I think this whole thing is crazy."

Jake stepped to her. "I'll give you that. But seriously, which of the two scenarios are more likely?"

A sudden consternation befell her face. "Jake, I don't know. I guess they're both crazy in their own unique and terrifying ways."

"Yes, but that doesn't answer the question. If you had to believe...if you had to give in and believe one or the other? Which would be easier?"

"Well, before I'd seen her, I would have believed the Frankenstein thing. But now that I've seen her, I'm not so sure. I mean, that girl, she's real. She doesn't move like a person, she doesn't move like someone who is just in a fake tail. She moves like she was born to move in the ocean. She has an ethereal quality, something unnatural to this world."

Jake knew exactly what she meant. He'd thought those exact things when he'd first started seeing Ariel. "I'll give you that too, but consider that she's been in the water her entire life. She'd be more natural in there than anyone you or I had ever seen. She'd be as natural as a dolphin, or a seal."

"True, but I don't know, Jake. I really don't know what to believe. I mean, you know me. I'm as opinionated as anyone. But in this case I have no clue."

He blew out an audible breath. "I have to shower."

As he stood under the stream of warm water, he had a hard time wrapping his head around things. It took him a long while to understand he wasn't crazy and suffering from hallucinations. But he had to wonder if his crazy conspiracy theory was even crazier than an actual mermaid.

After toweling off, he went back into the room. Ashley was fast asleep on the bed. He wanted to talk to her, but he didn't want to wake her. He quietly clicked off the lights and slid into the bed next to her.

Chapter 22

Ariel

Ariel didn't want to drink the special tea Father had given her last night, but he said it would help her to relax. It had. She didn't remember anything after the third sip. Now she was back in her bed, waiting for the sunrise.

She didn't feel any different, but Father said it would take several days before they knew if she'd started developing a baby. She had a vague memory of waking up in the exam room, but sometimes she had those dreams. There had been many times in her life when she'd required a medical procedure and Father had always taken care of it. That was why all mermaid guardians were doctors. That was the way it had always been, and that's the way it will always be.

Touching her belly, she wondered who would be the guardian of her baby. Father was too old to look after another one of her kind. It could be quite the undertaking while they were young. She was more than a handful as a child, always getting into mischief and causing Father to grow more gray hairs. He was completely gray now and she no doubt had a lot to do with that.

After a few deep breaths, she slid out of her hammock and into the water. Her arms were feeling a bit heavy so she went over to her box of things and took out her special balm that kept her upper body from becoming too waterlogged. It was important that she always kept her body treated because it was not made of the same skin her tail was. This was something all the mermaids had to do. It was just the nature of life.

After applying a good base, she pushed away from the rocks and headed out to swim a little. She was feeling a little dizzy as she went underwater and into her tunnel. It was a struggle to hold her breath until she popped out into the air.

It was a good day to see the sunrise so she headed out of the river inlet and into the open sea. The water was glassy smooth. Hardly any current or waves surged at her as she sped across the surface.

She felt something brush against her, and when she looked, two dolphins leaped out of the water to her right. "Hey guys!" she said as two more sidled up next to her.

She knew this pod well. They had been swimming these parts for as long as she could recall. "Did you guys come to see the sunrise?"

The lead dolphin—she called him Chester, after a character in one of her favorite books—made some quick chirps in response.

"It's going to be a good one today." She pulled

up when she was happy with the view. The sun was just starting to crest out of the sea. A beautiful orange glow overtook the world and spread like a beam across the horizon.

As she treaded water, the dolphin pod circled her, jumping and splashing as they often did. They talked to each other and maybe to her. And although she didn't claim to understand all their words, she could feel them. They knew when she was sad and they smiled a little bigger, squeaked and chirped a little longer, and brushed into her a little more softly. If people only knew how smart, amazing, and sensitive these beings were, they'd be worshiped.

The sun was up and the golden world above her was breathtaking. There were few things more beautiful than the sunrise over the ocean. Some people preferred the softness of the sunset, and she loved those too, but there was something about the start of a new day. Every new sunrise was like the bow on a newly wrapped gift.

* * *

Jake

Jake opened his eyes when he felt someone stirring around.

Ashley tossed some clothes at him. "G'morning."

He sat up, pawing at the garments on his face and cleared his eyes. He held up the black and blue board shorts and blue t-shirt with the white encircled CB on the front. "A Carolina Beach t-shirt? How touristy."

"I didn't put that much thought into it. It cost four dollars."

"You overpaid." He looked over her skin-tight pink stretchy shorts and curve hugging black thin-strap cotton top. He almost could not believe how beautiful she was. For several long moments, he could not gather his thoughts. Then he finally asked, "Where'd you get this stuff?"

"Down the street at the beach shop."

"They're open?"

"Sort of. I know Willie and Dina. They let me in to get this stuff. I knew you probably had no clean clothes. They didn't have a lot to offer."

Jake pulled on the shirt and shorts. They were both a perfect fit. "I do have some clothes in my car. I also have some at the storage unit."

"You have a storage unit?"

"It's mostly Cassie's stuff that we bought for the house. But I have some clothes there I couldn't fit into the room at Tom's." Jake moved his hand to his head. "Oh, shit. Tom."

Ashley faced him. "He doesn't know."

He shook his head. "No, he doesn't. I have to call him."

Ashley put her hands on her hips. "Okay, you do that. I'll go downstairs and get some breakfast."

* * *

175

Ashley

Ashley exited the elevator and went to the café that faced the beach. She placed an order for two veggie omelets and went over to grab some coffee from the pot at the self-serve bar. A man with large mirrored sunglasses, a red baseball cap, and a bad Hawaiian shirt smiled at her. He creeped her out, so she didn't want to smile back, but a little smirk came out nonetheless.

She almost turned around but really needed that coffee. While she poured, he watched her with the same creepy smile. It wasn't a shock, a lot of guys liked to look at her. She didn't usually wear a lot of makeup or flashy clothes, but it didn't matter. People always called her a natural beauty. And boys will be boys...the older ones were especially blatant.

"It's going to be a hot one today," he said.

Ashley didn't want to piss him off by ignoring him. And it was a public place. "That's what they're saying."

He eyed her up and down. "You're dressed for it."

"It's the beach life."

"Was a hot one last night."

"Yeah."

"You from around here?"

Ashley wanted to skirt the question, but didn't want to be outwardly rude. "No," she lied.

"Yeah, sure was a hot night last night, huh?"

"Yes, it was."

"It was like an inferno, a raging inferno."

"Huh?"

He stood with his back to the counter and crossed his arms. "Some people can't handle it when it gets that hot. That burning heat can really get to people who aren't used to it."

She glanced up at him, and uncomfortably uttered, "Yeah."

"You have to be careful when it gets that hot. You could burn up." He laughed oddly. "No amount of sunscreen is going to help with that kind of smoking heat."

Her pulse quickened to the point where she didn't want to make eye contact and give away her nerves. Usually she was a cool customer, emotions never obvious on her face or in her moves, but right now she felt like trembles and fear were just a cat scratch below the surface.

She finished pouring her coffee. "Okay, well...bye." She turned away back to the café where she prayed her order would be up soon. But as she stepped toward the counter, he took a step toward her and she decided to screw the food, and broke in a hurried pace to the elevators.

Once the door opened, she got inside and prayed he didn't follow. He watched her, smiled, but thankfully didn't climb in as the doors closed. She blew out a breath of sweet relief but her heart was still racing.

She got to the room, still clearly shaken as Jake looked at her and asked, "Are you okay?"

She fanned her face with her fingers. "That weird guy you saw at the beach that one time. What did he look like?"

"Umm, not real tall, kinda big-ish, but that's all I really remember. Why?"

"I don't know. Some weird guy down in the lobby." She realized just then she didn't even take the coffee with her, she left it on the counter next to the machine.

Jake put both his hands on her shoulders. "Hey, are you okay?"

"He said something. He said it was hot last night, like an inferno."

"So?"

"So? Well, the fire, he was talking about the fire."

Jake made a face. "Are you sure? What exactly did he say?"

She took a breath. It wasn't like her to get upset or rattled, but something about that guy got to her. "He said it was going to be a hot one today. I agreed. Then he said it was a hot one last night, he said it was like an inferno, blah-blah-blah…I dunno, Jake. It was weird. He knew something. I'm telling you he knew something."

Jake nodded. "Okay—okay."

"Don't patronize me!"

"Ashley, I'm not, I swear. I believe you."

"He just freaked me out, Jake. My creep-o-meter was off the charts."

He slid his arms around her and gave her a hug. "It's okay."

"What do we do? Maybe we need to go to the police?"

"And tell them what?"

"Well, someone is trying to kill us. They have to

care."

"They care, you talked to them. They know already."

"I know, but they have to care more than they've shown us."

"There's nothing they can do. It's all empty threats. They have no evidence, they have nothing. And this town doesn't have any sort of protection program. It's not like they're going to sit an officer outside the hotel."

She knew he was right. "I guess not. I know. Maybe I'm just being paranoid."

"As far as they're concerned, we're mixed up in something, and they think we had Mike killed. Technically speaking, we're probably still suspects."

Ashley slid away from him, walked over to the sliding glass doors, and sidestepped outside onto the balcony. She felt worse over Mike's death than she had to this point. Something about it all had just caught up with her like a freight train.

Jake was right. The cops didn't believe them, not fully. All the questions seemed to be more accusatory than sympathetic. Especially that one old cop, he was a real douche bag. He was convinced that some hit man they'd hired to kill Mike had turned the tables on them. They had no evidence of such things, of course. But they didn't act that way. She felt guilty until proven innocent.

"Are you sure you're okay?" Jake asked as he leaned on the railing next to her.

"I'm fine. I'm just feeling worn down. This is getting to me. I wish this would resolve itself. I'm feeling like a caged animal backed into a corner."

"I know."

She took a deep breath. "So what can we do?"

"We wait a few hours and we see if Ariel can help."

Ashley shook her head. "She can't help, she's a moron."

"Ashley, you—"

"No, Jake, you know it. She's too naïve to understand what's going on. She's like a clueless child."

"That doesn't make her a moron."

"Yes, that is the exact definition of a moron, Jake."

"Hey, she d—"

"Don't defend her, she's the whole damn reason we're in this mess."

"I'm not defending anyone. And Ariel might be naïve, but she's not malicious."

Ashley huffed. "Whatever."

"Hey, I'm on your side."

"Doesn't feel like it."

Jake said nothing. He just looked away.

Ashley knew she was being unreasonable, but she was mad. And the damn mermaid had everything to do with this mess. Her life was forever changed. Nothing was ever going to be the same again. "I didn't ask for this."

"I know, and I feel like shit about it."

"My life wasn't perfect but it was mine. Then you show up and now I feel like I've lost control of everything."

"Ashley, I'm sorry I got you mixed up in this.

I'm really sorry."

She let out a long sigh. "I'm not blaming you. I'm not mad at you. I'm just scared."

"Me too."

She was scared, about more than just the madman trying to kill them. She was scared because she was in love with this man she'd already been in and out of love with once before. She'd loved him so hard and had to bury those feelings under ten tons of concrete and steel inside a time capsule for all eternity. But here she was, here he was, the capsule busted open and the contents spilled into the deep unknown pool of a murky abyss masquerading as eternity.

Now the feelings were back and intertwined in this mess. It was stupid, she felt stupid...mostly because a part of her felt like she was going to lose him again to a freaking mermaid.

Chapter 23

Jake

Jake and Ashley waited on the rocks as the Fort Fisher breeze touched the shore. Jake could tell by the look on Ashley's face she was angry and worried. She had every right to be.

"You seem like you want to say something," he said.

"I'm just a little nervous."

"About anything in particular?"

"Oh, I don't know, maybe everything?"

"You've seen her before."

"Doesn't mean I'm still not freaked out."

"That's fair." The sun was on its last few minutes before it sank into the horizon at their backs. Jake looked down, and as if by some miracle he saw it, the barrel of his gun. "Holy shit!" He got up.

"What is it?" Ashley stood at his urgency.

"It's my gun."

"What?"

Jake got down on his knees, and then slid onto his stomach to stretch his arm down into the deep fissure between the rocks. With just the tips of his two longest fingers, he was able to hook the trigger guard and coax the black pistol back to his hand.

He held it tight. It was more than a gun. It was a symbol of his despair. He had formed a relationship with it unlike anything he'd known before. He'd accepted that this was the device that would end his pain, his life. In a distant and hollow voice he said, "I found it."

"You lost it?"

He nodded and smiled. "Yeah, the night I first met Ariel, I dropped it. I searched for hours the next day and couldn't find it."

Ashley touched his arm. "It's still hard to believe you were really going to kill yourself."

He looked off into the distance. "I just couldn't get my head straight. I was really messed up." He slid the pistol into his pocket, making sure the safety was on. "When she showed up here, all my problems just seemed so small. Even though I was positive she was a figment of my imagination. It woke me up. Just the shear idiocy of it all woke me up."

"At least something did."

"I guess sometimes burning down to the ashes is exactly what we need to find that phoenix inside every one of us."

She wrapped her arms around his waist. "I'm glad you did rise. I'm sorry I got so upset earlier."

"It's fine." He leaned in and turned to face her. "You've played no small part in this, Ashley. You were real, even if she wasn't. You made me realize there was something worth living for in this world, people who cared about me."

She placed a palm to his cheek. "I do care about you, very much."

The golden sky glow gave way to purple hues, darkening deeper with each passing minute. Jake looked down the beach, hoping the fishermen would pack up their stuff soon and head out.

"Do you think she'll come?" Ashley asked.

"She always has before."

"How does she know you're here?"

"I don't know. I think she just swims by and looks."

"Or maybe she's like some sort of psychic."

"That's funny, I asked her that."

"The psychic mermaid," she joked. "Coming to a theater near you."

"I'm not psychic," Ariel said from below them.

"Ariel." Jake took a few quick steps toward her. "You came."

"Of course. I always swim by this way at night."

Jake looked at Ashley and smirked. "You don't say."

"You weren't here last night," Ariel pointed out.

"I know. We had an incident. Someone tried to kill us again."

Ariel gasped. "I'm sorry."

"Ariel, we need your help."

"How can I help?"

"It's your father who's trying to kill us."

"He's not my father."

"You call him father."

"He's my guardian. Mermaids don't have fathers."

"Yeah, okay, whatever. We think he's the one trying to kill us."

"It's not possible. He's a gentle soul."

"He may be, but he could still hire someone."

Ariel huffed, clearly getting upset. "You're wrong. He wouldn't do that."

"Someone is. And no one knows we know about you."

"Father doesn't know, either."

Ashley offered, "I know this would be hard to accept, Ariel, but—"

"But nothing!" she fired back. "He wouldn't hurt anyone."

Ashley squatted down to get closer, her face clearly fighting the urge to anger. "Not even to protect your secret?"

Ariel dunked half her face into the water, covering her mouth. After a long silence, she eased her face above the water. "It's his job to protect me."

"He told you that?" Ashley asked.

"Yes. All the guardians are chosen to serve and protect. It is their directive."

Jake moved down closer, squatting next to Ashley. "Ariel, who chooses the guardians?"

"What do you mean?"

"I mean, if the guardians have directives, who gives them those directives? If it's a job, who's paying them? Who's their boss?"

Ariel shrugged and furled her brow. "That's a lot of questions I never thought about—I just figured they were chosen by fate or destiny."

Ashley rolled her eyes. "How simplistic."

Ariel made the first mean face Jake had ever seen her make. "Well, I'm simplistic. I've led a simple life. I'm sorry if that offends you."

"Hey," Jake eased out the words. "We're all on the same side here. Ariel, we just want to know what's going on. You can understand how scared we are."

Tears started to well up in Ariel's big blue eyes. "We're all scared. Life is scary and then it ends." She started to gather herself. "I found out my time on this Earth is almost over."

Jake frowned. "You mean...?"

She solemnly nodded. "Yes. Father informed me it was time."

"How does he know before you?" Jake asked.

Ariel shrugged. "It's one of the duties of the guardians. They know when it's time for all things."

"Ariel," Ashley asked. "Are you sure you're the only mermaid?"

"There is always only one."

"Yes, but only as far as *you* know."

Ariel looked confused. "I suppose that's true. If there are others, I've never seen them."

Jake stood upright. "It seems there's a lot of things we don't know."

Ariel nodded. "This is always the case with my world. In your world too. Mystery is the lifeblood through which all discoveries are made."

"How can we get into your house?" Jake asked.

Ariel searched the rocks with her eyes. "Why would you want to?"

"To find the truth."

"I don't understand what truth you seek. I've told you, Father is not the one trying to have you killed. He's a gentle soul, he'd never hurt anyone. I promise you that."

"Maybe so. But he knows who is."

Ariel pushed away from the shore. "I shall ask him." She sank under the waves and was gone.

Jake had never seen her so serious. He wondered if he'd done a bad thing. If he somehow put her in danger, he'd never forgive himself. But beyond that, he felt like he took away the one thing that made her so different from anyone he'd ever met. That one thing that made her so unique in a world full of hate and greed, it was her pure innocence. And he took that.

Ashley touched his arm. "We have to go get some clothes for tomorrow. We can't show up to a funeral looking like we just left the boardwalk."

Jake nodded. "I know."

Chapter 24

Ariel

After her morning swim and afternoon meal, Ariel surfaced in her pool just in time to see Father had walked into the room. She'd had all night to think of things to ask him, but as she saw him, she was disarmed of the feeling she'd had.

He was not dressed in his usual white doctor's coat, but instead in a black suit and blue tie with a pink flower fixed in the breast pocket.

"Ariel," he said. "You're home earlier than I expected."

"I didn't want to be out too late with the weather."

"That's wise of you. There's a storm brewing and the seas are going to be rough for the next few days."

"I know. I'm always careful."

"And if you are going to be with child, you will have to be even more careful."

"When will I know?"

188

"It will take a bit, a few days before we know."

"Why are you dressed like that?"

He pushed his glasses back up his nose and frowned. "I attended a funeral."

"I'm sorry. Who died?"

"Someone far too young."

"How'd they die?"

"A terrible accident."

"Oh, that's sad to hear." She looked forlornly at the gray through the ceiling.

He looked up. "Death is only sad if it serves no purpose."

"Did this person's death serve a purpose?"

He nodded. "Every death serves some purpose. The universe is an efficient machine in which no bit of matter or energy is ever wasted."

She sighed and nodded.

"Is there something on your mind, dear?"

Ariel swam over to the edge of the pool and propped her elbows on the deck. "Father, what would happen if I made a real friend?"

"What kind of a friend?"

"A human friend."

He looked up. "As you know, that could be a risky proposition."

"Would you hurt them?"

"Me? Heavens no."

"Even to protect me?"

He fixed his drooping glasses. "Why do you ask?"

She shrugged. "Just curious, I guess."

He pulled up his folding chair and sat next to the pool. "Humans don't like things that are different from them. We get scared and make rash decisions. You know all this, we've discussed this many times."

"I know. But what if there was a special one who understood?"

He nodded softly. "It could still come with complications. The people in their lives would never understand, and ultimately, it could get very messy."

"Who do you work for?"

He snapped his head back. "What do you mean? I work for me. You know that I have my own medical practice."

"No, I mean, who do you work for when it comes to me? Who chose you to be my guardian?"

His usually kind face turned sadder as a tired sigh seemed to drain from him. "I'm not able to discuss those things with you. You shouldn't even be asking such questions. What prompted this line of curiosity?"

"But why can't you tell me?"

"My dear, there is an order in life, an order of all things. There are those who make the rules and those who abide by them. Like everyone else, I am but a servant to a much greater master."

"What kind of master?"

"Is there more than one kind?" He stood from the chair. "Ariel, there is always a master for every life. You can be your own master in life, but there are certain strings of fate from which each of us must dangle. We answer to the universe, and to those that control the ways. Just as things have always been with your kind, things have always been with my kind."

He looked at her and she knew. His expressive face had never been so sad before. It was a profound sadness, which Ariel had seen only in others, but never in him. She wanted to cry, but didn't want to let him see it. "Goodbye." She turned away and jumped up into her hammock.

He walked to the steps, but he stopped. In the afternoon grayness he said to her, "Ariel, I wish things could be different for you. I wish they could be different for me. You're all I have left in this world. You're all the family I have, and when you're gone I won't have anything but my practice. I'm too old to be a guardian again, so someone else will have to take over this house and all that goes with it."

Ariel never realized that he didn't even own this house. The mermaid paintings that hung around the pool had always been just paintings, but now she wondered if perhaps they were history. The final pieces of her naiveté were draining away.

She glanced over to the wall. "Which one is my mother?"

Father didn't reply right away. After a long wait he finally said, "The one to which you are the most drawn. The heart knows." He spun slowly and started climbing the steps.

Ariel looked across the pool. It was too gloomy to see any details of the picture, but she knew it all too well. She'd stared at it hundreds of times wondering who the beautiful blonde mermaid was. She'd always called her mother in her mind, but never aloud or in true admittance. Now she knew…what she'd *known* all along.

* * *

Dr. Shepard

Bruce Shepard looked at his phone when it chimed. He didn't want to answer when he saw who it was, but it wasn't a choice he could make. "Hello."

"Is there any word on the baby?"

"It's too soon to know."

There was a long pause on the other end. "How's she doing?"

"Not good. What you feared is coming to fruition. She's just like her mother."

"That's too bad."

"Yes, it is."

"We should take the necessary precautions right away."

"I am."

"No, I mean we have to make sure everything goes as planned. We can't take a chance she loses the baby. You know this is not negotiable."

"I know how it works."

"I know you do."

"I know how to do my job."

"I know you do, and I know how to do mine, and my job is to make sure you do yours. And with that said, we need to secure things."

"You don't mean…?"

"I think you need to close the gates."

Bruce knew this was coming. "That won't be

good for the baby. Her stress levels will be too high."

"It didn't hurt her mother. She will make the right choices for the baby."

"But it is too long to lock her down. She's a free spirit, she's a good kid."

"Not that good. She's put me in quite the predicament with her behavior."

Bruce winced. "How is that going to play out? Never mind, I don't even want to know."

The long silence on the other end of the phone indicated just how angry he was. Finally, Bruce said, "If he'd done his job, maybe she wouldn't be so messed up."

"They have been lucky."

"Well, that's none of my business. You know I don't condone this method of operation."

"There's not another choice, Bruce."

"There's always another choice."

"No, there's not. And if I tell the council you said that, you'll be on their list too."

Bruce didn't care anymore. If the council wanted him dead, he'd be dead. In fact, he'd been guardian to two mermaids. There was every chance they were going to kill him anyway before he got old and senile and accidentally said something to someone. He would not give them the satisfaction.

Chapter 25

Jake

Jake walked up to Ashley as she sat on the concrete bench. The cemetery was empty now except for the two of them and a mostly quiet murder of crows. "You doing okay?" He slid his hand up her back and gave her a soft squeeze on the shoulder.

She nodded, wiping tears and faking a smile. "I'm okay. It was harder than I thought it would be."

"Saying goodbye always is."

She slapped her knees, "I'm a horrible person."

"Why?"

"I guess…I mean, I can't even say this out loud." She whispered, "A part of me is relieved."

Jake looked at her. He had an idea where her mind was but didn't want to say it.

"You're going to hate me," she said.

"Not likely."

"Well…" She appeared to be searching carefully

for the words. "In my head I was planning all this divorce stuff, and lawyer visits, and splitting of assets. And don't get me wrong, I did not want this."

"I get it," Jake replied. "That's a terrible process to go through."

"Yeah, but I'm a selfish bitch. I should not be thinking that. A man is dead, whether or not I loved him has nothing to do with that. I mean, I'd go through ten divorces to bring him back. You know what I'm saying?"

"Of course I do. The mind is a funny thing. We seek solace sometimes in the details and we look for positives within negatives. That's the nature of life. It doesn't make you a bad person. You can be sad for the death and relieved you don't have to go through a long arduous process at the same time."

"I guess it's weird that I don't feel worse. I feel like I should."

Jake just nodded.

She switched her crossed legs, smoothed her black dress. "I remember seeing you at Cassie's funeral. I didn't want to talk to you."

"No one did. All they did was say things they thought they were supposed to say, but none of it really meant anything. People don't really mean anything. They just say things. They were probably worrying about their drive home. I'm sure there are people at every funeral thinking that stuff."

"People did that to me today." She wiped a tear. "Mike's parents, they never really liked me anyway, and today they seemed so…I don't know…fake. All that stuff they said seemed so fake to me."

195

"They're pretentious assholes."

She laughed. "They probably think I killed him."

"Oh, there's no doubt," he joked, but then took a more serious tone. "Did you see the cop watching us?"

"I tried not to pay attention, but it was in the back of my head the whole time."

"He was looking for the proper mourning signs—as if everyone mourns exactly the same way."

She sniffled. "I guess they know what to look for."

"Screw them. They already cleared me. The gunshot residue test came back negative, they have nothing on us at all. Besides we know the truth."

She turned to face him. "What is the truth?"

"What do you mean?"

"We can't just keep waiting for whoever is trying to kill us to finally catch us out of luck." The gray sky rumbled with distant thunder.

He sighed. "Well, the good thing is that he doesn't seem to be bothering us in populated areas. He's opportunistic and takes his shots when no one is around to see him."

"For now. He's obviously a professional."

"Yeah," he agreed, "and he's missed us twice."

"Which means he's probably pissed off and more determined than ever."

Jake looked up to the sky. It hadn't started to rain yet, but it looked imminent. "It also means we're a more formidable opponent than he considered."

"That's not more comforting," she bristled. "It

probably means we're just full of dumb luck."

"But it tells me something."

Ashley shook her head. "It tells me our luck is going to run out."

Jake pursed his lips. "Or his is."

"Ha, that's stupidly optimistic of you."

Jake turned his palms up. "Isn't that a good thing?"

"Not really. And it's just hard to believe coming from a guy who had a gun to his head a week ago." She immediately changed the look on her face. "I'm sorry, I shouldn't have said that."

Jake rolled his lips inward. "It's a fair point."

"I still shouldn't have said it like that, though."

"I knew what you meant."

"I guess I know you did, you always do." She stood up, wiping the last tear off her cheek. "That's why I always liked you, Jake. You get me like no one ever did. It was hard when you stopped being my friend."

"I never stopped being your friend. But I did what I had to do to save my relationship, and yours."

She looked into his eyes, not a hard stare but a soft one that struggled to maintain steady. "I never wanted to be a source of anxiety for Cassie. She was my friend."

Jake started strolling towards the car, waiting a beat for Ashley to catch up. "Cassie was a great person, but she was always a little insecure with you. Not with anyone else that I ever noticed, but with you."

"There was a reason for it."

"I know. But she always said how pretty you were, and how lucky Mike was. It was almost like a little test she was sending up there to see how I'd respond. She wasn't dumb. She knew there was an attraction between us."

"Even though we never acted on anything, I think it must have been painfully obvious to anyone around us that we had some connection."

Jake knew she was right, but he didn't want to admit it. He always felt bad that Cassie was jealous when he was around Ashley. It was something he didn't even realize he was doing most of the time. But every once in a while he'd notice that he was gravitating toward Ashley over Cassie. It was ridiculous because Ashley was already married and he was engaged to Cassie and he loved her. It didn't make sense how he could love two people at once. That wasn't supposed to happen.

They reached Ashley's Mazda and she tossed him the keys. "Here, I don't want to drive."

Jake was about to duck into the driver's seat when he saw the man standing across the field beyond a frolicking murder of crows. He couldn't be certain from this distance, but it sure looked like the character from the beach. He had a similar stance as he leaned against a similar car.

"What is it?" Ashley asked from inside the car.

Trying not to draw attention to the fact he might have seen the man, Jake casually got into the car. "Look across the field there, past that tall headstone where those crows are."

Ashley scanned the scene. "I see him."

"I'm pretty sure that's our killer."

She nodded slowly. "I think that's the man from the hotel."

He glanced around. "Is there another way out of this place?"

"I don't think so."

Jake let out a groan. "We have to go right past him. And there's no one around."

"What can we do?"

Just as Jake was formulating an idea, another funeral procession started to pull up toward the gates. The standing man flicked his cigarette into the grass, got into his car, and drove out of the cemetery gates ahead of the hearse that stopped near the entrance.

Jake thought about waiting for the line of cars to enter, but instead he sped after the man.

"What're you doing?" Ashley asked.

"I'm going to follow him."

"Why?"

"To turn the tables a bit and see how he reacts." He took the turn onto the road so fast the tires groaned in protest. Heads of people parking near the gates turned to look at them as they sped off in chase.

"I don't like this," Ashley protested as they caught up to the dark blue sedan.

Jake pressed so close to the rear of the sedan that he could have bumped it with one more nudge of the gas pedal. Instead, he backed off just a bit but maintained close contact.

At first, the driver ahead did nothing in response, just maintained his course. But then he cut the wheel hard and turned down a side road. Jake was undeterred and followed.

As their surroundings started to grow more desolate, Jake had second thoughts. He was probably driving right into a trap. Not to mention terrible feelings about repeating history started to punch his mind like an angry boxer. The steering wheel was getting fatter, more slippery, and impossible to grasp. He stomped the brakes and let the lead car streak away into the thick pine forest.

The brake lights on the car ahead flashed as the back end reared up. Jake quickly pulled a U-turn and watched the rearview mirror. The car didn't swing around and follow them. Jake had no idea if he'd accomplished anything, but he wasn't second guessing himself either.

After a few seconds, his breathing returned to normal. He jumped when Ashley touched his hand on the gear shifter. She gave him a reassuring smile, but said nothing. She didn't have to.

Chapter 26

Ariel

Ariel awoke from her nap when she heard the most dreaded sound in the world. She'd only heard it a few times before, but she knew it well enough to fear it. Just like any caged animal, she feared the sounds of the locks.

In a rush, she flung herself out of her hammock and into the water, diving rapidly toward the tunnel that flowed to the seaway. In the murky light, she could see the gate closing. With furious determination, she used every bit of speed she could muster to get beyond that closing steel barrier. But it was too late.

She snared the steel in her hands, pulling until her muscles burned, but it was a useless effort. The gate closed with steady force against which she was helpless.

Slamming her palms into the bars, she let out a long underwater scream. Pushing her face close to the angled edges, she looked out past the end of the tunnel where the waters flowed. Part of her wondered if she'd ever swim in those warm currents again.

Spinning around, she slammed her tailfin into the gate, sending her back toward the pool...her prison. When she came up for air, Father stood at the edge of the water, dressed in his doctor's coat.

"Why?" she asked through saltwater tears.

He dropped his chin. "I'm sorry, Ariel."

"Then why?"

"I had no choice."

"Of course you do, you don't have to do this. There's always a choice, you taught me that."

"Sometimes there is no choice."

"That's a lie. There's never a time in life where there's no choice. You taught me, you taught me that—never—ever—ever—ever—ever."

He looked to the ceiling. "Choices define us. What we choose creates our character. The things we become are a direct result of each choice we make."

"Which proves my point that there are always choices, so why are you punishing me?"

"I'm not punishing you, dear."

"You locked me up like an animal in a zoo. Is that what I am?"

He sighed. "No, Ariel, you're—"

"But I am! I am a caged animal! I'm a freak! I'm a freak with a stupid fin!"

"Who told you that?"

"No one had to. I know what I am."

He turned around and pulled a wheeled cart near the edge of the pool. "It will soon be time to check and see if the baby has started growing."

"Is that why you locked me up?"

"This baby is very important."

Ariel couldn't help but wonder to whom the baby was so important. "It's my baby."

"Yes, she will be your baby, but someone has to raise her. Someone has to love her."

Ariel looked up at him. "What if it's not a she?"

He met her eyes for several long seconds, then looked away, and that's when she knew there was something so very wrong here. Exactly what it was she didn't know, but something was very wrong.

He shook his head. "It's always a girl. That's all mermaids can give birth to, females."

She felt like he was lying. "But what if it were a boy?"

"It never has been before."

"It would be a merman?"

"It's never happened before."

"You're lying to me."

He looked down at her. "I'm not lying. It cannot happen."

"You're not answering."

"I did answer. I have to go to work."

"And what am I to do all day? I can't get out to the garden, how will I eat?"

He slid a shopping bag off the cart onto the edge of the deck. "There's plenty of food here."

She fought back tears. "Why am I being punished?"

He frowned through a long sigh. "I'm sorry." He turned away.

"Is this because of Jake?"

He stopped in his tracks, he did not turn around, he did not move. He did not reply. But after several long seconds, he continued on his path. That's when she knew. His silence spoke a million more words than any words would have.

As Ariel watched him rise up the steps, anger started to build from somewhere in her gut. She'd never known anger like this. It was a new feeling. She clenched her teeth so hard her jaw began to ache up to her ears. Her fists involuntarily balled up so tight her trim nails dug painfully into her palms.

Even through her fury, she heard the quiet clank of the outside gate closing behind Father's car. He'd be gone until well into the evening. She was not going to be a prisoner, not again, not this time.

Planting her palms on the stone pool deck, she pulled herself out and onto the floor. In the only way she could, she slithered across the smooth stone until she got to the door, where a small, wheeled cart sat. She pushed the cart aside and reached up to turn the knob.

She knew there was something in here that could help. She'd seen them before and knew how they worked. Father brought them down here after he used them to get around when he twisted his ankle.

The aluminum poles stood there, leaning against the wall. She'd never tried to walk on crutches, but she'd theorized it was possible. Grabbing hold of the poles, she pulled them off the wall and onto the floor.

With one in each hand, she pulled herself up to her knees, and then with greater difficulty than she expected, completely upright. Being upright was incredibly unsettling. Her head started to spin, she felt sick. She tried to stay steady, but it was no use. She plunged forward quickly, smashing into a shelf, bouncing off that and into a mop and bucket.

The fall hurt, but she was undeterred and began to mount another effort. This time she did it smarter, with her back to the wall. When she got upright and the dizzy hit her, she let herself fall backwards.

She closed and opened her eyes several times, hoping to blink away the spinning. Adjusting her stance to get her tail in a more viable position, she realized it was not comfortable. The flipper at the end of her tail was not flat. It was difficult to stand on. But it had no real feeling in it, so she started to bounce on it until it sort of folded in front of her. It not only stabilized her, it sort of gave her a bit of a tickle feeling down in the end of her tail section, which on people would be their feet.

After leaning forward a bit onto the crutches, she was able to get the feeling of moving. It was only an inch or two at a time the first few steps, but after just a few more she started to get the idea. It started to feel okay.

Rather than heading straight for the steps, she decided to walk around the deck for a while, getting used to the feel of moving and turning. She had to do it now, because what she was planning was the riskiest thing she'd ever done in her life.

Chapter 27

Jake

Jake entered the shoddy roadside stand and looked around for Ridge. He didn't see him, but saw an attractive brunette girl propping a surfboard up against the wall.

She turned on a megawatt smile and widened her bright sea foam green eyes. "Hi, what can I help you with?"

He smiled back. "That's quite the cutter you have there."

"Yeah, she's a sweet stick, but the water was plowed today." She wiped her hands on her tight black shorts. "Are you looking for anything in particular?"

"I'm looking for Ridge."

Her smile instantly turned into a quiver-lipped frown. "Ridge is gone."

"Do you know when he'll be back?"

She just shook her head and didn't reply. Then she muttered under her breath, "He'll never be back."

Jake narrowed his eyes. "He doesn't work here anymore? I thought he owned the place." It wasn't until the end of his sentence that he figured it out.

She shook her head solemnly. "No, I mean, he's gone. He passed away."

"What?" Jake looked around with reactionary suspicion. "How? When?"

"A couple days ago. The funeral is Saturday."

Jake pushed the back of his hand to his top lip. "What happened?"

The girl walked behind counter, tears lined her face. "A freak accident."

"Accident?" Jake knew.

She wiped tears from the corner of her mouth that had run down her apple checks. "He was out early morning. Sets were rolling in."

"A surfing accident?" Jake interrupted.

"A boating accident. A hit and run."

"What?" Jake had a sinking feeling.

"Apparently a boat got too close to the surfers, hit Ridge and another guy named Dizzer."

Jake looked down. "I know Dizzer.

She nodded. "Dizzer made it, broken collarbone and wrist. Ridge wasn't so lucky, took a shot to the head. He never woke up."

"And they never found the boat?"

"Oh, they found it, but the owner wasn't there. He's a thousand miles away in Massachusetts. Someone stole the boat, took it for a joyride."

Jake blew a breath. "Holy shit…unreal."

"Oh, it's quite real." She turned up her palms. "This is all that's left of him. He put his life into this shop. Now it's mine and I don't even really want it." She broke down in tears, salted with uneasy, ironic laugher.

"Hey, don't cry."

She quickly bucked up reeled it in with a hard sniffle. "I'm okay, really. I'm fine."

"Was Ridge your father?"

She nodded. "Ridge—was Ridge, but he was my father…sort of, I guess. I don't know." She stuck out her hand. "I'm Jesse. How well did you know him?"

"You call your father by his name?"

"He was my sperm donor, he didn't raise me." She put her hands on her hips. "We just reconnected a few years ago when I turned eighteen and got the hell away from my psycho mother." She nodded. "Ridge was a lot of things that didn't make him parent material. But he was good, and smart. He didn't do drugs, he loved me, and he loved to surf." She bumped a balled up fist into the counter. "He left me this place and his house on the beach. I'm all he had."

"I only met him a couple times, but he left quite the impression on me."

She smiled. "He did that to everyone. Tourists he met a single time would come in here asking for him a year later. He just had that way about him."

"Yeah."

Jesse handed him a piece of paper. "Here's info on the funeral if you want to go."

"Thanks." The paper looked more like it was announcing a concert. "This is a funeral?"

"Not as much as a festival. Ridge wanted people

to have fun, to be thankful for their lives. Just because his was over didn't mean everyone else had to question their mortality with a boring black coat affair. He didn't want people to mourn his death. He wanted people to celebrate his life."

"That's a good thing, I guess."

"Why were you looking for him?"

"Umm, I just had talked to him about some stuff the other day and wanted to follow up on it. It wasn't a big deal."

"Well, if there's anything I can do."

Jake looked up on the wall at the mermaid picture. "Is that for sale?"

She turned to look. "The mermaid picture?"

"Yeah."

She looked at it closer. "Oh, that's for sale, I guess."

"Did he ever tell you about it?"

Jesse nodded. "Yeah, he did."

"He said it's real," Jake said under his breath, not really realizing he said it out loud.

"It's real, all right, from a real bad movie they shot here in the eighties."

"A movie?"

"Yeah, there was a movie called *Mermaid of the Atlantic*. It was a low budget deal, totally B-movie that never even made it to theaters."

"Huh, never heard of it."

"No one did. Ridge used to rent props. Half the stuff you see around this property was used in a movie at one time or another."

"No kidding?"

She pointed to the far wall at a large chair. "See

that ridiculously huge chair?"

"Yeah."

"That was from a version of *Alice in Wonderland*." She pointed to the other wall. "See that spaceship hanging? That was used in a movie called *They Came from Venus*."

"I didn't know."

"Yeah, there's all kinds of weird stuff around here. I guess that's the one thing about Wilmywood, there's no shortage of lame movie junk." She looked back at the picture. "Did you still want to buy the mermaid?"

He nodded. "Yeah, how much?"

She pulled it off the wall and flipped it over. "Huh, it says forty bucks. That seems excessive."

"No, it's okay. I'll pay it."

"You sure?"

"Yeah, it's fine." He handed her the cash and took hold of the picture. "Thanks."

"Thank *you*." She put the cash in the old-fashioned register. "I need all the cash I can get from this place."

Jake glanced around. "What're you going to do with the place?"

She shrugged slowly. "I don't know yet. I'm not really keen on sitting around here talking to tourists about movie props and random junk."

"You could hire someone."

"Yeah, I suppose I could. But this is prime real estate here. At least a dozen big names have come in here over the last few years trying to buy it from him. He never wanted to give it up. But I could sell the place and fund an endless summer of sand and surf for the rest of my life."

Jake laughed. "You probably could." Another customer walked into the store and Jake took that cue. "Okay, well, I'll leave you to your work."

"Thanks, and hey, if you need anything, you know where to find me. I hope to see you again at the festival-slash-funeral."

Jake nodded and ducked around the older couple walking in wide-eyed and smiling. He sat in the car and looked at the picture. If it was a movie picture, he should be able to verify that easily enough. He used his phone to look up the title of the movie on the movie database. Sure enough, it was there. The mermaid was played by an actress named Kate Marie Dixon. Though it was hard to tell, she could be the girl in the picture. It was plausible enough. But why would Ridge say it was a real mermaid? Maybe he was just saying what he thought Jake wanted to hear. Maybe Ashley was right and he was just trying to sucker him into paying a fortune for the picture. In a way it worked, he did pay too much.

Wheeling the car out of the lot, he headed back to the house to pick up Ashley. She'd finally been cleared to go back into the house. She wasn't going to stay, she was just packing up some things.

A shudder of guilt crawled up his spine over Ridge. He didn't know why, but it felt like his fault somehow. The fact it wasn't likely an accident didn't get past him for a split second.

First Mike, and now Ridge. If you add in Cassie and Paul, he'd left a string of death in his wake that he was starting to feel sick about. The overwhelming sadness of that idea nearly brought him to tears, but he had a sinking feeling that made him push the gas pedal to the floor and his old Volkswagen to its limits.

Taking corners at ridiculous speeds and screeching into Ashley's neighborhood, the panic in him didn't go away when he saw her car in the driveway.

Skidding to a stop, he jumped out and ran to the house, through the door, and into the foyer, where he called for her. "Ashley?"

There was no immediate answer, and he thought for sure his suspicions were confirmed. But then he heard her voice, "Help, help."

He ran around the corner into the kitchen. Her voice was there but she wasn't. It was just her phone, sitting on the kitchen counter playing an audio file of her repeating the words, *"Help, help. Help me please, Jake, help,"* over and over again.

But the tone was weird, there was no urgency in her voice. He picked up the phone and stopped the recording, bringing silence to the house. With one hand, he eased her phone into his pocket, with the other he eased out the pistol.

He'd never held this gun with the concept of shooting anyone but himself, but right now he wanted to kill. If something happened to Ashley, he didn't know if he could handle that. He didn't even want to try.

Creeping through the silent house behind the sights of the gun, he tried to control his breathing. His nervous tick of biting the inside of his cheek calmed him. He peered into the bedroom and saw some luggage, half filled with clothes. There were no signs of a struggle, which told him Ashley was playing it smart. It wasn't because she lacked the toughness and instinct to fight back, because she knew better.

After checking the last room, he hurried back down the steps and out to his car. He was about to call the police when Ashley's phone rang. He answered, "Hello?"

"Don't call the cops or you'll never see her again."

"If she dies, you die."

The man laughed. "I disappear for a living. You'll never find a trace of me or her."

"Just let her go."

"I can't do that."

"What do you want from us?"

"I don't want anything from you. I'm just doing my job."

"Who's paying you?"

"That's not important."

"It is to me."

"I don't have time for this."

"Make time."

"If you want to see her again, you'll do as I need you to do."

Jake was both angry and helpless at the same time. "What's the point, you're going to kill us both anyway. You've already killed two people."

There was silence on the other end until he replied, "What I've done is inconsequential compared to what I'll do."

"I think it matters a little."

"No, it doesn't. I do my job as contracted."

Jake paused then said, "What do you want from me?"

"I want you to drive down to Fort Fisher tonight at sundown. I think you know the place." The call ended.

Jake sat in the driveway, numb. He needed a plan and he needed it quickly.

Chapter 28

Ariel

The stairs were harder to master than Ariel expected. She gave up trying to climb them on the crutches because she feared a devastating fall. They were long, concrete, and curved with sharp edges on each step. One false move could spell disaster. She decided the best course of action would be to get down on her belly and slither up the steps. It was neither pretty nor fast, but it was effective.

At the top, pulling herself upright on the crutches, she surveyed the spacious room. She'd never seen this area before. She'd never been up the steps before. The only place she'd ever been was the medical office, which was off the pool area downstairs.

This was a new world. The house was very nice, and very clean. Something moved and scared her before she realized it was just a fluffy white cat. She didn't know Father had a cat. But there it was, clearly comfortable, but perhaps confused as to why

215

a stranger was in the house.

Spotting a small brown blanket on the piano bench, Ariel picked it up and managed to weave it around her body, tying it at her waist. The cat regarded her the entire time with curiosity but no real concern.

"Hi there, kitty." Ariel moved a few steps past the cat. It seemed wary of her clumsy gait.

Looking through the front door filled her with more dread as another short series of stairs awaited her. But she quickly formulated a plan as she twisted the lock on the front door and shimmied her way across the threshold.

At the top of the steps, she sank down to her backside and started to shuffle down the steps on her butt. It was much easier and more comfortable than it was going up, although these concrete steps were very coarse on the edges and dug into her hands with each slide down.

Pulling herself upright again at the bottom, she eyed the large white fence that bordered the entire property. At first, this didn't seem significant, but after a moment she didn't see how she was going to get out.

Approaching the gate, she eyed the lock, not sure how to open it. There was a keypad with eight numbers on it along with a red and a green button. Her only hope was that one of those buttons opened the gate at the end of the sidewalk.

With some trepidation, she pushed the green button. The gate opened.

All the excitement she'd considered wasn't even close to what she was feeling as she edged off the sidewalk and onto the street. She stopped to adjust the brown blanket wrapped around her body like a dress, making sure it was not going to fall off.

A shock of disorientation hit her as a car sped up the street toward her. The motion was hard to understand. It was fast, dizzying, and confusing. Colors of sky and grass soared through her vision. She stumbled and fell backwards, falling hard on her backside, hitting her head on the grassy area near the property.

In a bit of a swirled daze, she heard someone get out of the car and shuffle over to her. A man exclaimed, "Holy shit!"

She started to freak out, thinking he saw her tail. She looked up. "Jake?"

"Ariel?" He hovered over her, but didn't move right away. He seemed as shocked as she felt. With a shake of his head, he quickly bent over to help her up. "What're you doing?"

She steadied herself when he handed her the last crutch. "I'm running away."

He laughed.

"Don't laugh at me, Jake."

"I'm sorry. I just can't believe what I'm seeing."

"What're you doing here?"

His face turned more serious. "I came here to beat the hell out of your father and force him to tell me who has Ashley and where."

"Huh?"

"The man who tried to kill us—he's got Ashley. He's going to kill her, and probably me too, eventually."

Ariel nodded. "I believe you."

Jake nodded his head up at the house. "When's he coming home?"

"Not for hours."

"I'm going in."

"Why?"

"Why? Because there're secrets in there, there has to be."

Ariel hadn't considered anything like that. She just wanted to get out and get away. "I never considered it."

"I have." He started toward the gate, then turned and looked back at her.

He walked over. "Hold those crutches." He then swooped her off her feet and carried her through the gate, up the sidewalk, and into the house, where he put her back down standing, waiting for her to get the crutches situated.

"Thanks." It took her a moment to regain the breath he stole from her. There was something electric in his touch and something intoxicating in his smell that the water must have hidden.

He immediately started looking around, searching for something. She didn't know what to look for, or where to look, but she moved toward the desk and saw the pile of mail. It didn't look that interesting, so she just moved on to a notepad with some things sketched out in a language she didn't understand.

Jake had gone downstairs, and she was starting to feel a little weird. No one but Father or his colleagues had ever been down there, and for some reason it bothered her that Jake was down there without her. Not that there was anything down there that no one could see, it was just odd. She'd never felt anything like it before.

She was just about to move on from the desk when something caught her eye. It didn't look like much at first—it was just a sketch of a mermaid tail on a piece of tan paper. To the untrained eye, it wouldn't mean much, but to her it was interesting because it wasn't the same kind of tail she had. It had a different shape. The fin was more robust. For some reason she wished she had that tail. It looked like it might cut through the water with more thrust, more speed. She couldn't stop staring at it.

* * *

Jake

Jake stepped into a clean room the likes of which he'd never seen outside a hospital. It was what one might expect to see in a typical operating room. But as he approached the rear of the large space, something hanging on a rack caught his eye.

He approached the piece of material and touched it. It was grayish blue, heavy, and thick. It resembled dolphin skin. It looked like Ariel's tail, only slightly grayer. It felt odd in his hands, like skin but also like rubber. It was just a foot long piece, perhaps six inches wide.

He moved on, looking through a few other hanging samples of similarly constructed materials. He didn't know what to make of any of this. Perhaps they were patches in case Ariel was hurt. She did say she'd been injured before and needed surgery. Perhaps this was some sort of skin-graft material.

When he swung open a tall steel cabinet in the corner, he saw something even more confusing. Complete mermaid tails of various sizes and conditions. They were all similar but not quite identical. There was always some slight variation in each one. Exactly what this meant, he didn't know. Maybe they were like cocoons. Maybe as Ariel grew she shed her tail, like a snakeskin.

No matter how much he tried to rationalize what he was seeing in this room, something in his innermost being knew it was all wrong. But as he slid the drawer open on the tall blue filing cabinet, he didn't expect to see what he did.

* * *

Ariel

Ariel combed through the drawers of the desk and didn't find anything interesting. It just seemed like everyday stuff, bills, mail, and a flier about a charity dinner at the Starfish Lounge.

She looked up at the clock and didn't realize so much time had lapsed. But when Jake came running up the steps, she turned to face him. "What is it?"

He didn't hesitate. "We gotta go now."

He just scooped her up in his arms and started taking her out of the house. She was barely able to hold onto the crutches as he hurried through the door and down the sidewalk.

He stuffed her into the car so quickly she hit her

head on the roof. Jake apologized several times, hurried back around the car, and tore away from the scene.

Chapter 29

Jake

Jake wanted to get out of there as quickly as possible after realizing he'd probably tripped some sort of alarm when he kicked that door in.

"What's wrong?" Ariel asked. "Why'd we have to leave so fast? I think I'm getting sick."

He tossed a file onto her lap. "Ariel, it's all fake."

"Huh?" She opened the file.

"It's all fake. You're not a mermaid, you're a human."

"What are you talking about?" She started looking through the files.

Jake laughed. "It's all a freaking joke. You're just a person. You're a regular person stuffed into a synthetic mermaid tail."

Though she was seeing the same thing he did, he could tell she was having trouble. She threw the file back at him, sending the papers flying all over the car. "Is this some sort of joke?"

"Yes, Ariel, it's all a joke. It's a huge lie."

"I don't believe you."

"You saw it, it's right there."

"That doesn't prove anything. It's just pictures of my tail."

"What? What more proof do you need?"

He glanced away from the road to see the look on her face. It held a twisted expression of unimaginable confusion and grief. It was the look of finding out your entire existence was a lie.

"Ariel, I know this is hard."

She picked up a few pieces of the file and started shuffling through the papers again. "You don't know anything."

He pulled off the road and drove toward the water, pulling onto the sand under the pier. "You're right, I don't know how you feel. I can't even imagine."

She started to cry. "I don't even know what to say."

"I don't either. But they're liars, and murderers, and probably kidnappers."

She looked up from the papers. "Kidnappers?"

"Yes, Ariel. If you're not a mermaid, that means you had a mother, and a father. And who the hell knows who these people are or how they got you, or what their game is. But rest assured, I'm going to find out."

She pulled the blanket off her tail and touched her skin. "I'm a monster." The few tears in her eyes burst forth a huge flow.

"Hey, you're not a monster. Why would you say that?"

"When I was a little girl I read a book called *Frankenstein*. I loved that book. I read so many different versions. Every one I could find. I'm a monster, just like the monster in the books."

"No, you're not."

She punched her tail. "I was cooked up in a lab. I'm a freak." She punched herself over and over until Jake reached across the seat and stopped her.

He held her shaking wrist. "Ariel, look at me." She reluctantly met his eyes. "You're not a monster, you're not a freak. You're a human being and you know what that means."

She shook her head. "No, I don't."

"It means you don't have to die."

She searched the dashboard of the car and placed her hand on her belly. "My baby."

"Yes, *your* baby."

She looked at him. "But if I'm just a person, how did I become pregnant?"

"He must have done that in the lab too."

"I feel sick. I don't even know who I am."

Jake thought out loud. "I wonder what your name is."

"Huh?"

He looked at her. Her giant blue eyes looked so sad and glassy. "Your real name. It's probably not Ariel."

She leaned back into the seat. "Everything about me is a lie. It shouldn't surprise me that my name is fake too." She shrugged. "Who am I?"

"I don't know." He sighed. "But we need a plan. I have to get Ashley back somehow."

"What're you going to do?"

"Not me. We."

"What can I do?"

He met her eyes. "I only have one thing they want."

Ariel shook her head. "No, I can't go back there. If I go back, they're going to kill me. They're going to steal my baby and kill me."

He reached out and took her hand. "I'm not going to let that happen."

She sighed. "Please don't."

"But you're going to have to trust me."

She nodded slowly. "I do, I trust you."

"Okay then…now let me come up with a plan."

Chapter 30

Ashley

Ashley had never been in restraints. When her parents died, she felt like she'd been mentally restrained, unable to break free of the pain that haunted her for a long time. She'd always thought it was because she was at such an impressionable age when it happened. She was not mentally equipped to deal with such a tragic event.

There were so many *what-ifs* that day. She was supposed to go on that trip to New York with them. Her dad was just going on business, as he often did. He was a big executive with a pharmaceutical agency, so he often jetted around the world. This trip, like a few before it, he had the opportunity to take the entire family. They were going to see a Broadway show and visit the big museums. It was going to be great.

In the days leading up to the trip, Ashley started to not feel well. There was a cold virus running around her school, her number came up at the most inopportune time. She wasn't feeling well enough to travel, and they all agreed it was better for her to stay behind with her grandparents.

While watching the chaos develop on television, it never occurred to her that death would come for her family. She was worried, but so was everyone else that day. Even at eleven, she knew the chances they were in that spot at that time were remote. She had no way of knowing that they had gone to Windows on the World for breakfast. It all started to unravel when Grandma Nelly could not get either of her parents on the phone…and Dad always had his phone on him for work.

The days that followed were just one nightmare after another that seemed to drag on for weeks. When they'd finally gotten confirmation nearly two weeks later, it broke her apart in every way. It took years for her to rebuild. In some ways, she would never be whole again, but life had gone on, and she had triumphed above it all, just as her family would have wanted.

Now with one hand cuffed to the door of the car and one to the console, her fighting spirit was as strong as ever, but she refused to let it show just yet. She was going to hold all her cards until the right time. There was no way her life was going to end here without a wicked fight.

She could *not* be more uncomfortable. She could barely reach her nose to scratch it. There was no way she was reaching the itch on her left butt cheek, so she just kept moving the muscle to try to make it go away.

She looked over at the man keeping her captive.

His face was nondescript. He was wide-mouthed and tanned. His eyes were small and sharp. He was virtually expressionless, and other than a scar on the right side of his upper lip, he had almost nothing that would stand out if she had to pick him out of a lineup. Glancing down at the gun on the seat between his legs made her very nervous.

"Why're you doing this?" she'd asked before, but he never replied. In fact, she'd asked him several questions but not a single word was uttered in reply. Every once in a while he'd step out of the car, stroll around, and smoke while talking on his phone.

"Are you going to kill me?" He didn't reply of course. She decided that she was just going to start talking and not stop until he said something. "I wish I knew why you were going to kill me. Don't you think it's fair to tell someone why you're going to murder them? Can't you grant me that one tiny bit of human decency? You must be the one that killed Mike. He was my husband. Why'd you kill him? I was there when you did it. Why didn't you just kill me then?"

Finally, he turned and looked at her. He appeared as if he was going to say something, his lips parted slightly. But again he said nothing.

She'd hoped that talking nonstop would get him to crack and say something. She sighed. "Do you ignore everyone you're going to kill? How do other people handle it? I can't handle it."

She started to tear up a little. "I don't want to die yet. I'm too young. Life has so much to offer and I'm going to miss it all. I've never been to Europe.

I've never even been to New York."

With no fanfare he said, "I'm from New York."

Ashley looked up at him. "Is it nice?"

"It's an awesome shit-hole."

She narrowed her eyes. "Huh?"

"It's crowded, dirty, smells like diesel fuel. But it's the best place on earth."

"I guess I'll never find out. My parents died there. I haven't had the courage to see it. They were killed during the terror attacks. They just went to eat breakfast and boom...plane hits the building. They probably died instantly—at least that's what I like to believe."

He looked at her. His eyes softened ever so slightly, and Ashley felt like she'd connected in some way. So she poked at it. "Were you there that day? Did you know anyone who died?"

He had no reply again, but she could tell. He was human after all. But he was indeed going to kill her anyway.

* * *

Jake

Jake was nearly ready to give up on this whole concept. The plan was so risky, and probably stupid enough to get them all killed. But if they were going to die, at least they were going to die trying.

"I'm scared," Ariel said.

"I know."

She looked at him from the passenger seat. "Aren't you scared?"

He shrugged. "I'm mad, haven't had time to be scared."

Jake put the car in gear, and sped off toward the meeting that was probably going to end in disaster. At the very least, he was going to make certain that Ashley and Ariel got out of this alive. If it took his life to save theirs, so be it. He didn't tell Ariel that part of the plan, but it was the only part that really mattered. He was young and in good shape, he could hold off this guy long enough for them to get away.

At the stop sign of the rural road, he glanced down at his phone as the text message came through. He replied quickly to the text with a one word answer, and sped away again toward the beach.

The closer they got, the more nervous he became. He didn't want to make a mistake that would get someone hurt, and that was the part that made him the most uneasy. All the confidence he'd had just a few moments ago was getting harder to feel the closer he got.

To his right, the sun was almost set as he wheeled into the dirt parking area. "Here we go."

"Huh." Ariel laughed.

"What's so funny?"

"Nothing, it just looks so strange to see this view, to see the ocean from this perspective it looks so vast."

"It is vast."

"Duh, I know that, silly. It just looks so different."

He glanced to his left and saw the sedan. "Keep

down. I don't want him to see you."

Ariel slouched in the seat and smiled at him nervously.

Jake got out of the car, pocketing the keys and striding confidently toward the blue sedan. A cool ocean breeze hit his nose, to be chased away by choking humidity that could only be the tropical tip of the pending storm. The churning hurricane wasn't supposed to be a real bad one, but it was going to be enough to keep the coastal dwellers on edge.

As he got closer to the sedan he saw Ashley, a pleading look splashed her face as the man got out of the car and swung around the hood toward him.

"Don't come any closer," He said, holding his gun at hip-shot position. "Get your hands up."

Jake didn't comply. "I don't think so."

"Don't screw with me. I'll just kill you now and then kill the girl."

"I don't think you want to do that."

"Oh no?" He smirked. "Do you think there's some play here? Cuz you got nothing."

Jake took a few steps toward him. "Oh, I've got something."

"And what do you think that is?"

"Why don't you call your boss and ask him?"

The man twisted his head. "Huh?"

"Call your boss and ask him."

"What're you saying?"

"What part didn't you understand?"

The man scowled at him curiously. "I don't have a boss."

"You have one for this job." Jake smirked.

231

The man bore into him with a cutting stare. "Why should I do anything?"

"Because I have something very precious to him."

"Sorry to tell you I don't have a boss."

"So you're doing this for free? Is this your idea of fun?"

"I'm doing this for money."

"Then you have a boss."

The man's face hardly moved, but his eyes, they twitched and narrowed.

Jake laughed. "This is not some bluff. I'm dead serious. If anything happens to me, your bankrollers are going to be seriously disappointed in the outcome. And we both know that's not going to bode well for your future business. Now call him up and hand me the phone."

There was a long silence, a standoff. The waves made the only sound until a seagull screamed. With a short huff, the man finally pulled out his phone and dialed. "Yeah, it's me. I have something interesting here." The man nodded, and then he handed the phone to Jake.

"Hi there," Jake said.

"Who is this?"

"I'm the guy you want to be real nice to right now. I'm the guy who's got your precious little girl."

"Excuse me?"

"Yeah, that's right. I'll wait."

There was a long silence on the other end, so long that Jake was almost going to say something, but the man came back on. "You don't know what you've done."

"I know exactly what I've done. I know exactly what I saw in your house, Bruce—Belden—whatever the hell your name is."

"You don't know anything, my young friend." He laughed.

"I know enough. And here's how this is going to happen. You're going to tell your hitman here to let Ashley go, or I'm going to kill Ariel."

After another long pause, the man replied. "You won't kill her."

Jake knew that bluff would never work. "Okay, fine, maybe I won't. But you'll never see her again."

"You don't know the first thing about that."

"I know enough. And I know she'd be just fine on her own out there, a thousand miles away from whatever twisted game you people are playing."

"She wouldn't last out there, she needs us."

"You're going to kill her. And maybe you don't need her. But I know you need the baby."

There was another long silence. Then he replied. "Son, I'm only going to tell you this once. You have gotten so far under water that you can't even see the light at the surface. You're going to sink so deep and get crushed by the pressure of the sea."

"Look, all I want is Ashley. You let her go, and I turn Ariel over to you and tell no one what we've discovered. Your little secret can stay your little secret. I don't give two rat's ass hairs."

"You're lying."

"No, I'm not. All I want is Ashley and assurances that you will leave us alone."

"I can't do that. It's not my call."

"Then you talk to whoever's call it is and you make it clear. I want Ashley, and I want out of here. We will disappear and you won't see us again."

There was another long pause. It grew so long it turned into a delay. At several points, Jake wanted to say more, but he kept his mouth shut. It was clear the man was consulting with someone.

Finally, "Put Castro back on the phone."

Jake handed the phone back and waited.

Castro nodded into the phone. "Yes, I understand. That's feasible. Yes, fine. I will do that. Not now." He ended the call. He regarded Jake with a long look before finally turning around and heading back to the car. After a few seconds, Ashley was out of the car.

Castro held her by her arm, restraining her until she was within a few steps of Jake.

"Where's the freak?" he asked.

Jake smirked. "Oh no, not like this. It has to be on my terms or it's not happening at all."

"Then lead me to her."

"No chance."

Castro quickly reached out and took hold of Ashley's arm. "Then you'll get her when we get the girl. Girl for girl, like you said."

Jake looked at Ashley. "It's going to be okay. Trust me."

She nodded.

He looked back to Castro. "Fine, at dawn, north end of the beach near the curve. You'll see some trails, park by the first big trailhead. Rent something with four-wheel-drive."

Castro yanked Ashley backwards. She looked at Jake with pleas of sadness in her eyes but all he could do was nod a reassuring gesture. She was back in the car. Castro gave him one last nod before walking around to the front and getting in.

Jake went back to his car and got in. "It's done."

"They know I'm gone?"

"Yup."

"I guess the next part is harder."

"Yup."

He sent another text message. He was going to need something he could drive onto the beach and the Beetle would not do.

* * *

Jake helped Ariel onto the bed and set the crutches leaning against the cheap nightstand. "Can I get you anything?"

"No." She slid her hand across the bed. "I've never slept in a bed before." Then she eased back onto the pillows.

"Where do you sleep?"

"In a hammock over the pool."

Jake sat across from her on the other bed. The cheap motel was not that clean and didn't smell great, but he was able to park right in front of the room, away from potential prying eyes. "We need to sleep for a few hours."

Jake clicked the light off and flopped onto the bed. He wanted to sleep, but his mind would not relax. Ariel was humming quietly, a song Jake had never heard.

"Jake?" she asked.

"Yeah?"

Ariel was silent for a few moments. "That day in the water, did you like kissing me?"

Jake sighed. "Yes, I did."

"Would you do it again?"

Jake thought about the question, and part of him wanted to say yes. "I don't know, Ariel."

"Don't you like me?"

"It's not that."

"Is it because of Ashley?"

Jake did feel something for Ariel, but he didn't know what it was, and he didn't know what it meant. "Yeah, I guess."

"Do you love her?"

"I do."

"Do you love me?"

"Ariel, I...uh..."

"What I mean is, could you love me? I mean, maybe if life was different and if I was different, and things were different. I guess what I'm trying to ask is, am I loveable?"

"Of course you are." He wanted to be careful with his words, but he also wanted to speak the truth to her, she deserved that. "Ariel, when I met you, it was very special. I thought you were about the most beautiful girl I'd ever seen. You saved me and I did—I mean, part of me—fell in love with you. It was a strange time, and you were there for me and I'll never forget that."

"But we can never be. Even if I was not what I am."

"It's hard to say, because in a different time and

place, maybe we could be. But I love Ashley. I guess I always have." He searched the dingy ceiling with tired eyes. "Yes, Ariel, in another time and place. Yes, maybe things could be different for you and me."

Ariel sighed. "I'm happy for you, Jake. I really am. I just want you to be happy. I don't want you to be sad. If I die, I want to die knowing you are happy, I want that to be my last wish on this earth."

Jake felt that crush his chest. No one had ever said anything like that to him. "Ariel, you're not—"

"No, please, don't say anything else. Let's just go to sleep."

Chapter 31

Morning came very quickly and Jake didn't sleep well, but he was rested enough and the light outside the window of the motel indicated he didn't have much time. He sent a quick text message, and then swung out of bed before he realized Ariel wasn't in her bed.

A bit of panic set in before he heard the water trickle in the bathroom. He knocked. "Ariel, everything okay?"

"Yeah, I'm fine. I was just worried, my tail was dry."

"Can I come in?"

"Sure."

He opened the narrow door. "Do you need any help getting out of there?"

"I think I got it." She pulled herself up and swung her tail over the side of the tub in one swift move. Reaching across, she got the crutches and propped herself right up.

"Wow, you're getting good on those."

"Yeah, too good. I miss the water."

238

"We have to go now."

She took a deep breath and pressed forward. "Okay, I'm ready."

They quickly headed outside. Jake saw the white Subaru wagon was just where it was supposed to be, parked next to his Beetle. As promised, the keys were in it.

Jake picked this motel mostly because of its proximity to the north end of the beach. In just a few minutes' ride they were there, lumbering over the choppy sands as the waves crashed into the shore on their right.

Jake could see the longing on Ariel's face to be in the water as she looked at the waves. He didn't want to let her down, but there was every chance this was not going to end well for her or anyone.

The all-wheel drive wagon he borrowed struggled to maintain momentum in the sand and soon enough it got too deep to go slowly. But that was fine, he'd gone just far enough. Looking to his left, this was actually the perfect spot. The trails that led into the woods of Freeman Park were right there.

He walked around the car to Ariel's side. She was adjusting the blanket around her as he approached the window. "Are you ready?"

She nodded. "I'm ready."

He pulled open the door just as a small, silver SUV began rumbling up the beach toward him. "He's here." Jake sent a quick text and a GPS ping for their exact location.

The SUV drove up next to them and stopped. Castro got out and roughly dragged Ashley around as Jake helped Ariel upright outside the car onto her crutches.

Castro stuck a gun into Ashley's side. "Drop your pistol."

Jake moved his head back in surprise. "I don't have a pistol."

"You also don't have a good poker face. Now drop the gun and put the blonde in the truck."

"Let Ashley go first."

"Drop the gun first. Toss it into the sand over there."

Jake didn't think this part through. He needed the gun as part of his plan, but he knew there was a chance the plan would change. He reluctantly reached into the back of his cargo shorts and removed the gun from the small of his back, tossing it down in the sand near the tide. He just hoped the tide wouldn't sweep it away.

Castro pointed the gun at him. "Now, put the freak in the SUV."

Jake had to stall. He started to comply slowly when a screaming engine roared from down the trail toward them. They all looked as the grill and steel brush-guard of a huge black pickup truck rushed at them, slamming with reckless abandon into the silver SUV, sending it tumbling toward the water.

Using the moment of surprise, Jake moved quickly on Castro, going straight for the gun. He got hold of the man's arm but he was surprisingly strong. Jake was using every bit of strength he had to wrestle that pistol away. The struggle was epic. He kneed the man in the mid-section.

The gun was swinging wildly as shots started to

pop in every direction, just one after another pinging off the vehicles, thumping into the sand, and sailing out into the ocean to distances unknown.

There was no way Jake was winning this battle, but when two more shots issued and Castro dropped, Jake looked up to see Ashley behind the barrel of his discarded gun.

The driver of the large pickup jumped down to the sand. Seeing the small brunette get out of such a large truck seemed funny.

Jesse kicked some sand. "Fuck yeah, that was fun."

Jake was the first one to notice Ariel lying on the sand. At first, he just thought she'd dove to the ground to avoid the bullets, but then he saw the blood. He ran over to her, Ashley and Jesse quickly followed.

"Ho-ly shit!" Jesse exclaimed. "You weren't kidding. This is real."

Jake slid his arms under Ariel's body. He glanced around. "Jesse, get us out of here."

Ashley said, "I know where to take her."

"No." Jake hurried toward the pickup bed. "It's too risky."

"It's too risky to take her back to Dr. Shepard too." Ashley dropped the tailgate on the big old Ford.

Jake eased Ariel up into the bed and jumped up with her. He met Ashley's eyes. "Go tell Jesse how to get there."

She pushed up the tailgate and hurried to the cab. The big Ford chewed up the sand, spitting it out behind them as Jesse piloted them to the paved roads.

Chapter 32

Jake waited somewhat impatiently in the small foyer. He trusted that Ashley knew what she was doing. "You sure we can trust this guy?"

She smiled. "If you can't trust Garrison Booker, you can't trust anyone. This man should be dipped in bronze, covered in gold, and adorned with a crown of diamonds."

"How come I've never heard of him?"

"He moved here from the Bahamas a year ago."

"But he went to medical school, right? I mean a real one, not some online college or something."

"He went to Cornell. He was born in Jamaica, raised in Haiti and Botswana, and moved to New York when he was sixteen to go to college here in the States. He ran his own private practice in the Bahamas for fifteen years before ending up here. He owns a non-profit called Island Kids that treats sick kids all over the Caribbean."

"Why did he end up here?"

"His girlfriend is a Marine from Jacksonville."

"Makes sense, I suppose." Jake slid deeper into

the plush chair. "How'd you meet him?"

"My car broke down on the bridge at Snow's Cut. It was raining ice, and he's the only one that stopped to help me. As soon as I saw those big brown smiling eyes, we became friends."

Jake felt a little better after hearing about Garrison. It's not that he didn't trust Ashley, he did. But he had to consider everything, it was just in his nature. He was a born cynic, which by definition meant he looked for the potential fault in everything.

"Hey, Jake, let me ask you something."

"Sure."

"How come you dropped out of school?"

"Who told you I dropped out?"

"You did."

Jake fought back. "Well, I never technically dropped out, I just didn't go to graduation. I still got my degree a year later."

"How come you didn't go?"

He shrugged. "Wasn't really a point. My parents weren't going to show up, they were off on some wild tangent at the time. I guess I just didn't want to be bothered with it all. It was dumb, anyway."

"Yeah, I guess they all are."

"I mean, I already had the financing lined up for the bike shop by my second year, I didn't really need to finish anything. I was eager to get the shop up and running, so I had to get home to do that."

"Mike always thought you were too soft to make it in the real world, so you opened a bike shop. I assure you I didn't agree."

"I mean, I've wanted to open that bike shop

since I was fifteen. I only went to college so I could learn how to actually run a business. I didn't want to fail right out of the gate."

"You didn't."

"Not at first. I guess I have now."

Ashley shook her head. "Not true, Jake. The shop has only been closed for a few months. You could get it up and running again in no time."

"I suppose I could."

"I'll help you."

Jake smiled. "You want to work at a bike shop?"

"I could still teach my real estate classes on the side."

"I guess so."

"C'mon, let's do it." She leaned forward. "We could get that thing ripping again. Let me be your partner."

Jake nodded. "Okay, if we live through this, you have a deal."

The doctor came out of the white door, drying his hands. Ashley wasn't lying, he did have the biggest, kindest brown eyes Jake had ever seen. They were only slightly lighter than his dark chocolate skin, which was only slightly lighter than his short black hair. Jake and Ashley both stood.

Garrison smiled. "She's going to be okay." His accent wasn't thick, but it was there. "The bullet missed mostly everything. It was easy enough to remove."

Ashley reached out and hugged the doctor. "Thank you so much."

Jake reached out a hand. "Yes, thank you, Doctor. This is a debt I can't repay."

Garrison smiled. "Of course you can. Every debt can be repaid. It matters only what the lender wants in return."

Jake wasn't sure where he was going with this. "Umm...I—"

"Relax, man." Garrison lightly tapped his shoulder. "I'm kidding with you." He tossed the paper towel in the garbage pail. "She's sedated now, probably won't be awake for a couple of hours."

"But she's going to be okay?" Jake asked.

"She's going to be fine." He made a face. "But what you were telling me, about the tail. I did...well...let me just show you."

They went into the room. Ariel was lying in the bed. Her tail was propped on a low table with a white sheet underneath it. Garrison pulled back a tiny piece of her tail from around her hip. "This is not something I've ever seen before."

Jake looked at it. "I don't know what I'm seeing."

"This tail—it's a shell, yes—and it is a biosynthetic-like material of some type. But it doesn't appear to be synthetic in a true sense. There's a membrane underneath that is part of her, it's grown into the tissue. I mean, this isn't something that you can slip on and off."

"So," Ashley asked. "What're you saying?"

"I don't know. But it's not some simple fake like you said it was."

"No, I don't imagine." Jake stood upright. "These people have big bucks, whatever they made her into, they probably spent a fortune."

"Well, that's just it," Garrison offered. "I don't

know how you could make something like this."

"But I saw the plans for fitting the tail onto her legs."

"I don't know what you've seen, but this is not something that was fitted on. This is something that is part of her, like your skin is part of you."

Jake asked, "Are you saying she's actually a mermaid?"

Garrison turned up one side of his mouth. "I am not able to say such a thing. I am saying that this tail, this skin, it is not manufactured. It is grown. It has viscous properties, and it is alive. It may not have nerve endings, but it is definitely not rubber, Kevlar, neoprene, or something made in a factory. I do not know what to make of it, but it appears to be skin. Unlike any I have ever seen on a person."

"But you have seen it?" Ashley asked.

Garrison nodded. "It is very similar to the skin of a sea mammal, a dolphin or manatee perhaps. Only it is more pliable, softer and much thinner than those animals. You could no sooner remove this skin than you could remove human epidermis."

Jake shook his head. "But I saw diagrams, plans, and sketches for tails."

"I can't speak to that," Garrison replied. "I can only tell you what I see right now. And what I see is something extraordinary."

Jake nodded. "I know who does know something. And we're going to see him. Right now!"

He turned out the door, waiting for Ashley to follow. It took her a few long seconds, but by the time he reached the sidewalk, she was running after him.

"Jake, wait."

He turned. "You're not stopping me. I've had enough of this."

She held his arm as she spun in front of him. "I don't want to stop you. I just won't let you go off all half-cocked."

"I'm not. I'm fully in control here. I'm just tired of the lies."

Just then, his car pulled up with some strange dude behind the wheel, and Jesse in the big pickup behind. She'd gone back to the motel to retrieve his car.

She jumped out of the truck as Jake approached. "Thanks again, Jesse."

"No problem."

The tall lanky guy climbed out of Jake's Volkswagen and tossed him the keys. Jake caught them and headed to the car.

Jesse chased him down. "Hey, cops are all over that place, man. They're going to be looking for someone, I'm sure."

"Anyone see us?"

"I can't say. But I mean..." She nodded to Ashley. "You killed a dude on the beach. So, like, I'd stay low for a while."

"Don't worry," Jake assured her. "That man will never be identified, I'd bet my life on it."

He got into the car and waited a beat for Ashley to climb in before he tore away from the scene.

* * *

They arrived at Dr. Bruce Shepard's home. Jake didn't wait a second before he went up to the gate. He expected to have to break in, or jump the fence, but much to his surprise the gate swung open before he even had the chance.

Ashley followed him through the white iron fence, and when they approached the door, a short, thin man with kind eyes and a sad, drawn face opened the door. His salt-and-pepper hair was dry and frizzy, and his face was old, not distinguished.

He waited for them to enter. "I've been expecting you." He closed the door behind them.

Jake didn't reveal the fact he had a gun in his pocket, but he was fully prepared to do so if he had to. "You have every reason to expect us."

Bruce walked into a library. Tall shelves stacked with books on dark wood surrounded them on three sides. "Please have a seat."

This was all too cordial for Jake. He was angry and wanted this to be anything but cordial.

Bruce sipped from a white coffee cup. "Is my Ariel okay?"

"She's not your Ariel. Not anymore."

"I raised the girl since she was a baby, she's every bit my daughter."

"You treat your daughter like a lab experiment?"

"I treat her how she must be treated for what she is."

Jake said nothing, but he knew for certain that this man was not the one he had spoken with on the phone. His voice was tired and lagging in speech.

Ashley huffed. "You're a sick bastard."

"You don't know what you're talking about. Not

the first thing about of what you speak, my young friend."

"That girl is fighting for her life right now," Jake exaggerated.

"Because of your incompetence, Jake, because you stole her from her world."

"No, Bruce, because you pushed her too far. I came here to confront you and found her on the street."

The old man sighed. "I know. I saw the surveillance video."

"Then you know you pushed her too far."

He sipped his cup. "I know. I told them it was too much. Ariel is not like the others, she's much more headstrong. She's smarter. She definitely knows what she wants. Perhaps I read her too many books as a child, but she had such a voracious appetite to learn and read. They will blame me for it."

"Who are *they*?" Ashley asked.

"Oh, they are who they are."

"What do they do?"

"They do what they do."

Ashley laughed. "You don't want to tell us, I get it."

"I'm just a humble servant to the master."

Jake interjected. "What master?"

Bruce sipped his drink. "When Ariel was a little girl…when she first came to me, I knew she was special. She was just like her mother. I'd raised her mother from a baby and she was a real pistol, as they say. But much less adventurous than this Ariel."

"Wait," Jake said. "So you didn't steal her?"

"Steal her? Young man, why would you say that?"

"I know she's not a mermaid. I saw the tails in the basement."

Bruce smirked, then let out a loud belly-laugh that would have rivaled even the best department store Santa Claus. "Young man," his voice was still peppered with laughter, "you don't know anything. Not even the first thing. She is not like you or I in any sense." His laughter trailed off. "She's much more special. What you saw is not any sort of explanation. Something that appears to be one thing might turn out to be something, or some thing or nothing or no thing."

Jake looked over at Ashley, she had the same puzzled look. "I don't know what anything you're saying means. But are you trying to say all that crap Ariel told me is real?"

Bruce took a longer swig of his drink. "Everything I've told her is everything I know. I've never knowingly lied to Ariel."

"Well, what the hell is really going on here?" Jake asked. "Is she a real mermaid or not?"

"Do you believe she is real?"

"I don't know what to believe." Jake leaned forward. "I believed she was real, then I saw your little laboratory and figured it was all fake. I mean, if she's real, why does she need more tails? What the hell is real?"

Bruce sipped his drink and leaned forward to match Jake's posture. "The illusions of your reality are always tied directly to the reality of your illusions."

"Huh?"

He raised his cup. "We create the world we want. Our minds are the most powerful thing in the universe. We control the destiny that we think is so random." He paused, folded his arms over his legs. "There is a small aspect of chance which we cannot control, of course. But ultimately, everything we do, every choice we make, is the ruler of our reality."

Jake bit the inside of his lip. Something about those words hit him too hard. "That's bullshit."

Bruce smiled. "I'm sorry?"

"Things happen to us. We can't control everything."

"You don't think so?"

"No."

"You don't think you could've driven another way home that night?"

"Huh?"

"You don't think you had a choice not to chase those kids that night?"

Jake swallowed hard, his voice bit back. "How do you know about that?"

"They know everything about you, Jake. They know everything about you, Ashley. They know every move you've made and have an answer for you at every turn. There is no place in which you can hide. There is nothing you can do to change what's going to happen because you chose this fate by pursuing this to the end. You can fight it with all your life, but it will only cost you more than you have in the end. You don't want this fight, you cannot win it."

"Why?" Ashley asked. "How can they know about me, and why would they want to?"

"It is their world and we are just in it. I've come to the end of my time here. I've decided to go out on my own terms and not let them be the ruler of me. I wanted to quicken my end. It is not…" Bruce's face changed, it went slack. His eye started to twitch. He clutched his chest, and fell forward onto the ground with a sickening thud.

Ashley stood up, slowly reaching her hand to her mouth. "Oh God."

Jake sank down to one knee and reached for Bruce's wrist, but pulled his hand back. It would have been nothing but a formality. He knew.

Ashley gripped the top of her head with a fistful of hair. "What the hell just happened here? Did he just kill himself?" Ashley walked in a circle around the room. "This is crazy—this is crazy—this is crazy."

Jake stood. "This has gone about three turns past crazy." He picked up the coffee cup, a white substance still floated in the murky black.

"Jake, what are we going to do? I'm really getting scared. I feel like we're losing this fight."

Jake sighed and glanced around. He knew she could be right. The better part of his brain said to get the hell out of this place immediately. "We should go."

Ashley took a step, then stopped. "You don't think they know where we took Ariel?"

He shrugged, half jokingly offering, "They probably have a GPS tracker on her."

They shared a look of paranoid concern.

Jake rushed out of the house, jumping into his car in one motion and turning the key. Ashley was quickly next to him. With screeching tires, he ripped away from the curbside. He drove in a hazardous panic. Memories of that night, the accident, all came flooding back, but he didn't dare take his foot off the gas. This time he wasn't recklessly chasing a car full of jerks out of anger, he was hurrying to try to save a life or two.

In front of Garrison's office, he brought the car to a skidding halt on the gray asphalt. He barely remembered to put the car in park before he was heading full speed toward the front door.

As he ran into the office, he expected the worst and he found it.

Garrison was dead on the floor, there was blood everywhere. It looked like he'd been stabbed twenty times. On the floor next to him was someone Jake recognized, but didn't know. His name was Hops, and he was a local homeless man who spent much of his time drifting around the island, hopping from one part-time job to the next, and one cheap motel to another. They called him Hops because he was constantly drunk and always looking for booze. He too was dead, but not a scratch on him; in his hand, a large hunting knife.

As Ashley entered the room with her hand over her mouth, his first instinct was to push her away from seeing the carnage, but it was too late. She'd seen it already and looked ready to vomit.

He quickly ran into the exam room, and as expected, Ariel was gone. Nothing remained of her except the brown blanket she'd used to wrap herself.

"She's gone?" Ashley stated more than asked, even though it sounded like a question.

Jake pinched his nose. "Another random coincidence."

"They're cleaning up their mess. And obviously anyone who saw that mermaid has to die."

He shook his head. "No, not just anyone who saw her, but anyone who knows what we know."

She glanced back toward the bodies and bit back tears. "I can't believe this. This is my fault. I should have never brought her here. Garrison is dead because of me."

"No, Ash, he's dead because of some psychotic clan of mermaid creators, or whatever the hell she is, or they are. I don't even know which way is up anymore." He thought he felt crazy before, now he just felt like a rubber room was probably a better option than this insanity.

"Jake, maybe we should just get out of here."

"Yeah, I don't want to be here when the cops show."

"No, Jake. I mean we should get the hell out of town. My cousin has a condo down in Florida. It's usually empty this late in the summer. He spends the winters down there from Michigan. The keys are with the local real estate office and I'm on the VIP list."

As smart as that idea sounded to preserve their lives, he felt the compelling need to find Ariel. Ashley must have known what he was thinking.

"Jake, maybe you can't save her."

"Maybe I can." He stormed out of the office and

got into his still running car.

The second Ashley's ass hit the seat he sped off, annoying her as she struggled to click her seat belt. "Jake, slow down please."

He was so mad he didn't want to.

"Jake, saving Ariel is not going to bring back Cassie."

Like a slow, creeping scorpion, he felt the insect legs of realization feeling their way all through his body. Maybe she was right. Maybe that's exactly what he was doing. He slowed the car and pulled down one of the sandy beach access roads and stopped. "Is that what I'm doing?" he asked more to himself than Ashley.

"That's what is seems like to me." She twisted to face him. "Do you love her?"

"Cassie?"

"Ariel."

He thought about the question. He kind of did, but not in the traditional way. It was something different. It was a connection unlike he'd ever had with anyone or anything. And maybe it was directly tied to what she was. Or maybe it was how they'd met.

"Well, do you?"

He met Ashley's eyes. "I don't know."

She looked visibly upset. "You either do or you don't, Jake. It's not a trick question."

But it kind of was. "Not like I love you."

She formed an uneasy smile. It was one of those half-scared and uncomfortable smiles. It was the kind of smile that told him he'd just said the right thing but at the wrong time.

He huffed. "It's hard to explain."

"Hey, I get it. She was there for you when no one else was." She looked away.

"Yeah, but...I don't know."

"Yeah, you don't know. Because other people were there for you, Jake, you just didn't take our help. My help. I was there for you from the start and you didn't see it."

He nodded slightly. "I know, and I'm sorry. I don't know what else to say. I was in a bad place, Ashley. No one could help me, and I didn't want help. The truth is I was addicted to the pain. I was addicted to the hurt. And if I stopped hurting, I felt like Cassie was gone forever."

"Jake, Cassie is gone forever. She's gone from this world. Nothing you do will ever bring her back."

He clenched his teeth so hard his jaw started to hurt.

"She will always be part of you. She will always be in your heart. Nothing can take that away."

"I know all that."

"You know it, but you're not living it. It's that simple."

"Oh, thanks for that. Now you tell me," he quipped sarcastically.

"Stop being an ass. You know what I mean."

"Yeah, but how...how the hell do I live it? It's not as easy as just that."

"Yes, it's exactly that easy. It's just that easy. You have to make the conscious choice to do it. You have to be better than the tragedy."

"What does that even mean?"

"It means that what happened does not define you. It's not a part of you. It's just the way it was. It was a tragic event, but you're better than that one event."

He didn't say anything he just mulled over what she'd said.

"Right?"

He shrugged.

"Say it, say you get it."

"I get it." And he did. For the first time he got it. He glanced over the top of the dune, stretching his neck to see the ocean. But couldn't quite make out the waves, so he got out of the car and climbed the dune, ignoring the protected dune sign and stepping over the hump.

When Ashley stepped up next to him, he said, "When I was first getting used to the idea of Cassie being gone, I would purposely make myself cry. I don't even know why. I don't even remember what motivation I had for it. But I would just want that pain so I could feel close to her. It felt like if I didn't cry, then I didn't love her anymore."

"That's not the way it works."

"I know. But it seemed logical at the time."

"Of course it did. Everything seems logical while we're doing it. That's why people make mistakes all the time. And I'm not saying you were mistaken to feel that way. But you were mistaken to keep feeling that way. You have to just acknowledge the feelings and then move on. You can't dwell on them for weeks and months. I mean fercrissakes, Jake, you were going to end your life over it."

"I don't do well with guilt."

"I can understand that. Guilt is a funny thing. Unless you're a sociopath, you're going to feel some guilt over things. In some cases, you're going to let it linger."

Jake shot her a look. "What did you say?"

"I said you can't let it linger."

"No, the part about being a sociopath." Something she said brought back the conversation they'd had with Roger Pender.

"What about it?"

He turned to step in front of her. "Roger Pender."

"Who?"

'Roger Pender, Dr. Shepard's former partner."

"What about him?"

"He said something very interesting about sociopaths and their behavior."

She shook her head. "So what? Where're you going with this?"

Jake didn't know how he knew, but it just came to him that Roger Pender knew more than he'd led on. "He did lie to us."

"How do you know?"

"It was something he said. Or rather how he said it." Jake jumped over the dune and ran to the car.

Chapter 33

They stopped at the gate of the community and the guard asked them whom they were there to see. After Jake said the name, the man at the gate turned and punched a combination into the pad and they drove in.

After parking, they headed over toward Roger's building. The woman at the table smiled at them. "Hi, how can I help you?"

"We're looking for Roger Pender?"

"Hmm, I'm not sure where he's at today."

Jake pointed. "He lives in that building, right?"

"I'm not sure which one he's in this week."

He narrowed his gaze. "I don't understand."

The woman shrugged. "He stays wherever he wants, we don't keep track."

Jake laughed. "So the residents just roam about from place to place?"

She chuckled. "No, not the residents, only the owner."

Jake looked over at Ashley. "He owns this place?"

THE MERMAID

The woman started going through her phone. "Oh, you'll find Mr. Pender over at the library." She pointed a skinny arm. "Head over to that brick building. He's doing a reading. He reads Shakespeare twice a week to the residents."

Jake swung the wide door open and stepped into what looked like every generic public library he'd ever seen. It had the modern side filled with computers on desks, and the traditional side with low shelves of books spread out wide for easy reaching.

They turned the corner of a curved wall and came upon a crowd of about twenty people dispersing. Roger Pender was packing some books into a briefcase when Jake approached. "You almost had me fooled."

Roger looked up at him and cocked one brow. "Pardon me?"

"You really almost had me fooled. That whole innocent act, it was compellingly done. You had me convinced."

Roger stood upright. "Son, I don't know what you're talking about."

"Bullshit, you old bastard—you know exactly what I'm talking about."

He set his stance and eyed Jake. "The last man who spoke to me like that had to have his teeth surgically removed from the back of his throat."

"Take your best shot, old man. I don't think you've got the balls." Jake readied himself, but he was a little nervous. Roger was probably in his early sixties, but it was clear he was strong as a bull. Jake also had a suspicion that the old guy knew how to throw a punch.

Roger turned a half smile. "Son, I'd tear you apart and leave nothing for the buzzards."

"You don't scare me."

He laughed. "Then you're not only ignorant, you're also stupid and lack the self-preservation skills and situational awareness required to live long enough to enjoy the wisdom I have acquired."

Jake sighed. "Look, I don't want to fight you."

Roger laughed. "Now that's the smartest thing I've heard you say yet."

"I just want to know the truth. I want this insanity to stop. And I don't want you to sit there and deny what I'm talking about. I know you know it."

"I'm afraid you know nothing."

"I know too much, and whoever pulls the strings in your little group wants me dead because of it. They've already taken Ariel. And since you're going to kill us anyway, why not share the truth? I just want to know she's going to be okay."

"Son, you don't deserve anything, because I don't know what you're talking about."

Jake laughed. "Okay, have it your way. But know this. I may be just ignorant and stupid enough to blow this shit wide open. And it might kill me, but it might also kill you. So you have to ask yourself, Roger, is that the way you want to play it? After all, I've already come further than anyone else has."

Roger stared at him, but Jake didn't waver one bit in his face. He kept cold and hard, and the poker face was not going to crack. Roger must have seen the desperation in his eyes, or something in there that caused his aggressive posture to sink just enough.

Ashley stepped up to him. "Dr. Pender, we don't want to cause any more trouble. We just want to live. We've both lost so much we don't want to lose everything else. But know that we will fight back with everything we have. And although it might not seem like much compared to you, the first rule in any battle is to never underestimate your enemy. I assure you. I'm not one to be underestimated."

She stepped smoothly between the two men. "Look, whatever the truth is, it can't be worse than what we've already assumed. And it's not like we can prove anything, anyway."

Roger looked at her. For a long time his hard stare didn't change, but then, it did. His glare softened with a long sigh and a slight turn of his head. He slid his phone out of his pocket and turned away from them, taking a few quick steps out of earshot in front of some rolling carts filled with books.

Jake looked at Ashley. "How do you feel about this?"

She nodded. "I feel good. I feel like if they wanted to kill us, they would have already."

"Yeah, but it's not for lack of trying."

Roger swung around toward them, sliding his phone into his pocket in one motion. He approached and folded his arms over his chest. "Okay. You two perhaps have earned the right to know the truth. But there are conditions."

Jake nodded. "We have conditions too."

"You're in no position to make any demands."

"That's fair. But I want a guarantee that no matter what happens, Ashley comes out of this alive."

Roger stared at Jake for several long seconds before sliding his hand into his pocket, and pulling out his wallet. Only breaking eye contact for a brief second, he finessed a business card into his fingertips.

"Meet me at this address in two hours. We'll proceed from there."

Jake glanced at the card and looked to Ashley, who shrugged. They spun away and headed back to the car.

* * *

After parking in the dirt lot of the old marina, Jake looked out over the water and wondered where this was going. As suicidal as he was just a few days ago, dying was the last thing he wanted now. He especially didn't want anything to happen to Ashley. He didn't want to admit it to himself, even though he'd already said it, but he was in love with her all over again. Perhaps he'd never stopped loving her and he felt sick to his stomach that something might happen to her.

He glanced down the street when he heard an engine humming, but after a second it became clear it was not on the road, but in the water.

A medium sized pontoon boat, white with a faded yellow canopy and even more faded yellow outriggers, chugged slowly toward the rickety dock that led away from the marina.

Jake stepped up onto the weathered planks and turned to hold out a helping hand to Ashley. She was not the kind of girl that needed the hand, but he offered out of habit and because it was the chivalrous thing to do. He'd gotten used to doing those sorts of things for Cassie. She wanted a hand, doors opened, and things that used to define male chivalry. Jake didn't hate doing those things, in fact he kind of liked it.

The skipper piloting the boat wasn't familiar, but Roger Pender sat in the far corner, his elbows propped on the rail behind him and his arms spread like a waiting vulture.

Stepping over the small gap between the dock and the deck, he glanced back to make sure Ashley made the step as the boat drifted slowly by the dock.

Roger motioned for them to sit. "I told you there are conditions to this. That was not lip service."

Jake sat. Ashley sat to his left away from Pender. "I'm sure."

"I've discussed this with my colleagues and we've agreed. There have been too many deaths. We don't trust you. We should just kill you."

"You're wise not to trust us."

"You've surprised us at every turn. To top it off, Ariel is threatening to harm herself and her baby if anything happens to you. We can't have that, not with the amount of time we've invested in her. And we may have an offer for you that will keep everyone happy."

"Is that right?" He looked skeptically at Roger.

The boat chugged out of the open water and down the wide inter-coastal waterway. The tall, sandy hills rose up majestically on both sides and helped to usher them down into the river waters.

At the apex of a long, slow turn, the skipper turned the boat down a narrow, blind inlet that led them down a waterway just wide enough for the outriggers to scrape by the vegetation. The soft rustling of foliage was usually a soothing sound, but for some reason in this case it bothered Jake. Perhaps it was because he thought something sinister waited down this serene path.

Just as the trees and shrubs felt like they were closing in on them, it opened up to reveal a huge house. It was three stories, stone faced, and wrapped with porches and patios around the whole structure. It was not in impeccable repair, but it certainly didn't look like a dump.

There weren't any other houses around, it was as isolated as any on these inlets that Jake had ever seen. He wondered if it could even be seen at all from the road. Looking beyond the house, he couldn't even see any roads in the distance. He knew the landscapes around these waters, but this place seemed almost foreign.

The skipper stopped the engine and let the boat drift silently between the two docks that reached out into the water until it bumped softly into the tires.

Roger stood and stepped effortlessly onto the dock without a word. Jake let Ashley go first before he followed. At the end of the dock, they traversed a few steps up to a winding sidewalk of cement lined with red bricks.

Roger turned and faced them. "What you are about to see only a handful of people outside of the organization have ever seen. You have to understand that trying to blow the proverbial whistle on something like this will result in nothing for you. You will accomplish nothing, you will prove nothing, you will save nothing. We have the power to take your life, without killing you. You will only make yourself look like a fool."

Jake nodded. "I understand. But why're you trusting us?"

Roger sighed. "Ariel is making life very difficult for us. We don't want her to come to the same fate as her mother."

"What fate was that?"

Roger turned, "This way."

They headed up the sidewalk and entered the large house. The foyer was spacious and open, yet effectively clinical. Jake felt like he was walking into the future. Everything was white marble tile and gleaming surfaces.

Roger motioned with his hand. "The things you think you know about us, about the world, may not be the same once you leave here. And the fact is, not every question you have will be answered."

"Then why are we here?"

"You're here because you've eluded your demise more times than anyone has in the past. You're here because Ariel still wields some power over us. You're here because she loves you." He turned and walked down an arched hallway.

Jake followed, gauging the look on Ashley's face. It wasn't one he'd seen before, but he knew what it meant. It was a universal look that all women could muster when needed.

They entered a large room, at the center of which was a small holding tank where Ariel lay in a sling of sorts, her tail dangling in the water. She wasn't awake.

"What's wrong with her?" Jake asked as they approached.

"She's in a sort of medically-induced suspended animation so she doesn't hurt herself."

"Why?"

"She became increasingly agitated and had to be subdued. We can only keep her in this state for a few more hours due to the risk of harm to the baby. This is why we decided to bring you into the fold. She asked for you."

"What is all this?"

Roger walked them to a wall on the far side, where several very old pictures hung on the wall. He pointed to the top left. "Gretchen Korolev, she was the first one. Born to a Russian mother and father unknown, she came out severely disfigured. The bones in her legs were fused together, her hips were malformed. Doctors tried everything but the mother was told she would die."

"I don't understand."

Roger pointed to another picture. "That was Anna Companelli. By the time she was born they had a name for the condition, they called it Mishkaylev Syndrome after the one prior."

"What is it?"

"It's a genetic mutation. It's like nothing anyone has ever seen before, and even in this day and age we don't understand what causes it."

Ashley touched a picture. "They're all so beautiful."

Roger nodded. "They are indeed."

"Who're their parents?"

Roger smiled. "As I indicated, not every question would be answered. There are things even I don't know."

"This makes no sense," Jake stated. "So these babies are born with this syndrome and you turn them into mermaids? This is twisted."

"Do we turn them into mermaids? Or are they born that way?"

"You put tails on them and toss them into the water. For what reason? To perpetuate a myth?"

"Myth and legend are rooted in truth. There is nothing so callous going on here as you suggest. They are not born like you and I...they are different."

Ashley spoke up. "You steal their lives, force them to have babies, and kill them. What the hell do you mean there's nothing callous going on here? That's the very definition of callous."

"There are things you don't understand. We do as we've been commissioned."

Jake rolled his eyes. "Passing the buck again. To whom this time?"

Roger's poker face didn't flinch. "We save them."

Jake tilted his head. "What's to stop me from killing you and taking Ariel out of here?"

"Son, you'd not get a minute down the road before being crushed into dust. You wanted to know the truth, now you know."

"I don't know anything. All I know is that something twisted is going on here and you still won't tell me who's in charge."

"Who's in charge doesn't matter as much as the fact that they are."

"It matters."

He motioned one hand. "Look around. You've seen only a tip of this operation. There are millions upon billions of dollars at work here. The untold fortune behind this is not what you think it is. It's more money than you've ever seen. And more power than you can imagine."

"But why? To what end?"

Roger walked along the wall, looking up. "A legacy perhaps? A fascination with the unknown? It's anyone's guess."

Jake laughed. "This is insanity. Are you telling me some eccentric billionaire has been taking little girls born with some crazy unknown syndrome and turning them into mermaids for his own twisted pleasure? Is that what you're telling me? Because I want to get this straight."

"It's far more complex than that."

"Well, why don't you break it down for me so I can understand it."

"There are things we are not meant to understand."

"This is bullshit!" Jake exclaimed. "You're telling me everyone goes along with this not knowing who they're working for or to what end? I don't buy that, Roger. You're a smart guy. You wouldn't agree to this unless you knew exactly what it was all about. So quit jerking our chain and tell us what's really going on here."

"I told you what I'm allowed to tell you. It has to be enough to satisfy your curiosity. There are certain things I'm unable to pass along to you for various reasons."

"Like what?"

"It's not that simple."

"Everything is as simple as the truth, Roger."

"The truth is an illusion of time. All things we know of truth today will be but myth and legend tomorrow. And all things that were myth and legend of the past will be truth again someday."

Jake sighed. "Why are we really here?"

"Because, Jake, the organization is impressed with you, mostly with how much you cared. They want you to be the next guardian."

Jake let his jaw drop open like his mouth was expecting words his brain would not send.

"That's right," Roger reiterated.

"But I'm not a doctor."

"No, Jake, not the guardian for one of the mermaids, the guardian for all of them. They want you to run the entire organization. You'd be working directly above me. You'd be my boss."

Jake looked to Ashley, she was just as flabbergasted as he was. "I don't understand. I don't know what to say."

"What's to understand? With all that has gone on, we have not had the time to vet a replacement. Under normal circumstances, one would be chosen ahead of time. However, our friend Castro made some flawed errors in judgment. Losing Dr.

Shepard was not part of the original plan, but things went sideways a little bit and he left us on his own terms. He was on the committee set to choose a new president."

"Why me?"

"Because you're the perfect choice."

"No, I'm not. I'm really not."

He handed Jake a set of keys. "These are for the house where Dr. Shepard was living, and for the front entrance to this facility. You will watch over Ariel until the baby comes, and then you will live here and oversee the operations. We will train you on everything and give you a handsome salary beyond your wildest dreams. And of course Ashley is welcome to join the organization. You asked how people do work and don't ask questions? Well, you're going to find out why."

Jake stood there slack-jawed. He didn't know what to say.

Roger fixed his hair. "I'll leave you two alone to talk for a few minutes while I take care of a few things."

Chapter 34

Roger

Roger Pender entered the office where the willowy woman waited. She was no less than six-foot-three and built like an exotic runway model, tall and lanky beyond explanation with absurdly large blue eyes and a tiny mouth that barely moved when she spoke. To him her name was only Avaroush.

"Is he on board?" she asked in her slight British accent. Her voice was soft and direct at the same time and had a somewhat mechanical resonance.

Roger nodded. "It's an offer he can't refuse."

"Very well. If he plays along, he lives today. If he refuses, he and his lovely girlfriend will die today."

"Keep your enemies closer," Roger added.

Avaroush turned to face the large window that overlooked the inlet. "We don't have enemies, Roger."

"I'm still not completely certain he can be

273

trusted."

"It doesn't matter. We only need him for a few months, because once the baby comes, he and the girl will be disposed of."

"We don't want to underestimate those two. They've proven quite lucky."

She moved with refined grace toward the window. "Luck is only a manifestation of ability and desire. There is no possible way to estimate the level of one's desire until the immediate need to overcome adversity crosses into their path. People have the ability to rise to the occasion, constantly surprising their peers, adversaries, and themselves. It is the human station in life to trample upon the ground of mediocrity until greatness is required."

Roger considered himself an intelligent man. He graduated medical school at the top of his class. But when Avaroush started spewing her philosophy, he often felt like he was mentally inadequate. He had no idea how old she was, but she didn't look a day over thirty. Something, however, told him she was much older. It was not surprising she was so skinny; he'd never seen her eat anything except raw vegetables and fruits.

He stepped toward the door. "I trust in the plan."

"As you should. The universe has a way of taking care of what needs to be."

He turned and headed out the door.

* * *

THE MERMAID

Avaroush

Avaroush turned to face the wall where her twin sister appeared from a small door. Ayallta was identical in every way to her twin; there was not a single distinguishable difference. They often worked independently under the same single profile. No one knew the other existed, as they'd never appeared in the same place at the same time in public.

Ayallta lowered her large eyes. "I don't believe Mr. Pender is of use to the operation any longer."

"Agreed. I think things have become increasingly difficult to sustain on our current course. We may need to cleanse. It is no longer fluid. Far too much attention has come."

"Mother and Father would approve this course of action if we feel it is the correct solution."

Avaroush flexed a long finger and pointed to the window. "It is time, perhaps, to move on for now. This baby must be protected at all costs, she is the purity. We cannot risk a single thing. But for now we keep the operation on track. We will make the decision when the time is appropriate and not before then."

Ayallta nodded. "We will know. And what is to become of the Pender man?"

Avaroush turned a tiny smile. "He will become…special."

"It is too bad. He has served us well for a long time."

"Too long. We have to remember next time to choose better. We were too clinical with this operation, it was too unfeeling."

"I agree, we need a more caring approach next time."

Avaroush smiled. "We have made our decision then?"

"Yes, my sister, I believe we have."

* * *

Ariel

Ariel woke up, but would quickly fall back to sleep again. It was a weird sleep. It was not restful, but it was peaceful. It almost felt like she was in some sort of dream but could still wake up, but couldn't. Each time she would wake, a woman in a white mask would come over and twist a dial on the tall green canister by her side.

When she would sleep, she would dream of kissing Jake. They were walking around. In the dream, she was human with legs, and it was wonderful. Also mixed in was a strange place she'd never been. It was a peaceful place with a pinkish sky and perfectly crystal blue waters. The dreams would come and go quickly.

She was familiar with medical procedures, over the years she'd had many. Sometimes Father would tell her it was minor, and other times he'd tell her not to worry but when she woke up something would be different.

Now that she knew the truth, she wondered just how much of it was real at all. A new dream started to rise in her. She was swimming in the ocean with her favorite pod of dolphins. Snaking in and out of their wakes, she loved to jump in behind them. She could speed so much faster when they were breaking the water ahead of her. It made her feel invincible, like nothing could catch her.

Although the dream seemed happy, sadness overwhelmed her as she wondered if she'd ever get to swim in the ocean again. She felt like there was a chance they'd never let her go. They were just going to take her baby and kill her. She no longer believed that she would die. She no longer believed anything Father had told her. If one thing was a lie, it was all a lie.

As she tried desperately to keep her mind sharp while pretending to be asleep, the woman in the mask eased over and twisted the knob. It sent Ariel into a deeper state of sleep.

Chapter 35

Jake

Jake entered the large home and dropped his bag of new clothes on the tile floor of the foyer. He took a deep breath and looked back at Ashley, who was striding across the threshold. She plopped her bag next to his.

"I don't like this," she said.

Jake just shook his head. "No...not at all." He took a few steps in and turned back to her. "But for now, we're going to have to play along."

"Should we?"

He shrugged. "I don't think we have another option."

"See, that's what I'm talking about. They made an offer we couldn't refuse, quite literally, knowing we wouldn't."

"Yeah."

"But what if we had?"

He met her eyes.

She stepped closer to him. "What if we had,

278

Jake, then what? Where would we be?"

"I don't know." He knew she was right, and he knew this whole thing stank, but only a complete fool would pass it up. Only a fool would believe there was no hitch involved. A fool would also sell his soul to the devil.

Ashley sauntered through the archway into the kitchen. "Well, the place is nice."

"It looks nice, but it feels all wrong."

"Well, any new place is bound to feel that way."

He shook his head. "No, it's something more than that."

She spun to face him, walking slowly toward him. "Are you okay with this?"

He sighed. "I don't feel good at all, but if we don't look after her, who will?"

Ashley slid her arms around his waist. "No, I mean are you okay with this?" She pulled him closer. "With this!"

He raised his shoulder and held it there as he thought. "Of course, why wouldn't I be?"

"We're going to be living together here, not in the way we'd both probably wanted—under some bizarre circumstances. Technically, we've never even been on a real date. I just wanted to make sure. I mean, we haven't really had the time to talk about feelings and things like that. This whirlwind has taken us away and thrown us into a world we're probably not even meant for."

"None of that matters. We don't have to talk about anything. You know how I've felt about you for years. Just because we couldn't be together doesn't mean I never wanted to. This feels as natural and normal as anything I've ever known. Yeah, the circumstances are whacked out of reality. But what can we do? We just have to go with it for now and worry about all that other stuff later."

She slid her arms up his shoulders and bent him down to her. "I just wanted to be sure. You know me. I never assume anything. I always need verbal confirmation. Maybe that's very female of me, I don't know. But be patient if I ask stupid questions."

He laughed. "Of course. And be patient with me if I don't get it. I'm historically kind of clueless with women's feelings, so never be afraid to speak up. Don't assume I know anything either."

"Okay. So open lines of communication will go a long way."

"A very long way."

The sound of a vehicle hummed up the street. Jake knew it was probably the van bringing Ariel back to the house.

He walked over to the window and pulled the shade up. A white van waited at the gates near the driveway. He pushed the button near the door and let the gate swing open. The van crept down the slight hill of the drive and around the back.

They both went downstairs. Roger Pender was at the side door looking through the glass. Jake pulled the door open and Roger entered. He pushed his back into the door, holding it open so the two men dressed in white lab coats could carry Ariel into the room where they unceremoniously dumped her into the water in one motion and turned away.

Roger walked over to her. When she surfaced, he

squatted down. "Now, Ariel, you're going to behave. Right?"

She nodded. "Yes."

"You have to take care of that baby. She's your legacy." He stood and nodded to Jake. "I'll be in touch." Then he walked out the door.

Jake squatted down. "Are you okay?"

Ariel propped herself on the edge of the pool and looked around suspiciously. "I'm fine for now. As long as those creeps are gone."

"Well, they're gone. But they'll be back every week to check on you and the baby."

Ariel looked behind her. "Am I still locked in?"

Jake shrugged. "I have no idea."

Ariel quickly went underwater and kicked away across the pool, disappearing into a tunnel of which he could only see the leading edge.

"Jake." Ashley kicked off her flip-flop and dipped her toe into the pool. "We need some sort of exit strategy."

He rose up, crossed his arms. "Like what?"

She twisted her lips to one side. "I don't know yet. But we've got some time to think about it."

Ariel popped up out of the water. "The gate is closed."

Ashley questioned, "There's a gate?"

Ariel spit some water. "It's in the tunnel that leads to the river."

"Was it locked before?" Jake asked.

"Yes, they'd locked me in when the baby started growing."

Jake could see the look on her face and it was an uncomfortable consternation. "Maybe I can talk to

281

them and see if they'll open it."

"It must open and close from somewhere in this house," Ariel offered. "Because Father used to do it."

Jake glanced around and then started to make his way around the pool area. "Where did he go to do it?"

"I don't know."

Jake scoured the pool area but didn't find anything. He then went into the thin door near the rear of the pool next to the door that led outside. After opening the flimsy door, he found the circuit breaker box and several other buttons.

He flipped and clicked every button in that room but nothing worked. With a palm-up shrug, he walked back toward the pool. "I'm sorry. I'll ask them."

Ariel looked visibly nervous. Then she swam around in an angry circle of kicks and slapping arms. Jake couldn't help but be reminded how young she was in terms of mental maturity.

Ashley squatted down at the edge of the pool. "Hey, we'll work this out, no need to get all huffy."

Ariel stopped, treading water a few feet away. "You don't understand. I've been so bad they're going to punish me. I'm just a baby maker to them now."

Ashley glanced up at Jake but didn't say a word.

Ariel looked around. "Where's Father?"

Jake sighed. "They didn't tell you?" Jake shook his head. "I'm sorry, Ariel."

"Father is gone, isn't he?" She looked despondent.

"Yes, he is."

Ariel nodded. "I knew he was gone. I felt it."

"I'm so sorry, Ariel," Jake said. "I wish things were not the way they are."

Ariel smiled. "Father used to say that same thing to me. He loved me a great deal. I wish you'd have known him during happier times."

"Me too. I wish we all would have known each other during happier times."

Chapter 36

Jake woke up before the sunrise and heard the whimpering. Once his eyes adjusted for the low light, he sat up. Ashley was still sleeping silently next to him.

As he leveraged himself to the edge of the bed, Ashley rustled and tugged at the blankets. With a gravel voice she said, "What time is it?"

Jake got to his feet. "It's early."

Ashley groaned her way to a seated position. "Is that crying I hear?"

"Yeah." Jake slipped his feet into his flip-flops and headed down the hallway toward the stairs.

As he got closer, the crying turned more into a moan. He turned the corner, rubbing his eyes awake while navigating the new-to-him dynamics of these curved concrete steps. The second he saw Ariel, he knew something was wrong. "Are you okay?"

From her hammock, she turned to look at him, tears streaming down her face. She just shook her head slowly but didn't say anything.

"Ariel, what's wrong?"

"Something's wrong with my baby."

"What is it?"

She moaned. "I don't know, it just hurts so bad."

Ashley came shuffling toward them from the staircase. His face must have given away the gravity of the situation because her posture changed from casual to urgent. "What's wrong?"

Jake shrugged at her and widened his eyes. "I don't know."

Ashley touched his arm. "Where's your phone?"

"Upstairs, nightstand."

Ashley turned, and in a few quick steps, disappeared up the stairs.

Jake stooped over to the low-slung hammock. "Ariel, where does it hurt?"

Through tightly clamped eyes, she just shook her head with a soft whimper.

Ashley returned, already talking on the phone. Roger Pender had given them his emergency number in case they needed anything. She ended the call and said, "He's on his way."

The next twenty minutes went by excruciatingly slow for Jake, but no doubt, they felt like a lifetime for Ariel. Those minutes paled in comparison to the minutes that clicked by once they arrived and took Ariel in the exam room.

As he faced the pool, looking up at the rising sun through the glass, Ashley slid her arms around his waist from behind. "You okay?"

He nodded. "I'm fine."

"I hate to be the voice of reality here, but…"

Jake nodded over his shoulder to her. "I know."

"If something happens to that baby."

"I know."

"Jake, we need a plan quickly."

He turned to face her. "Ashley, I want you to know that I love you."

"I know you do."

"Whatever happens next, just know that."

"I love you too, Jake. I always have."

After another few moments, Roger Pender stepped quietly out of the exam room into the pool area. The look on his face said it all. No matter what this man was, no matter what insanity this whole mermaid thing concealed, Jake knew that Roger did truly care about that baby. He wasn't even sure how he knew that, maybe it was just intuition, maybe it was the fact that at his core this man was a doctor.

"How is she?" Ashley asked.

Roger puffed out his formidable chest and flexed his rugged jaw. "She lost the baby."

"I'm sorry," Jake said. "She must be devastated."

Roger's expression went cold. "I have to go. I'll be in touch."

As he turned, Jake stopped him. "Wait."

Roger turned slowly. "Not now."

"Hell yes, now." Jake insisted. "So what happens?"

"We're taking her for more tests."

"Tests? For what?"

"I have some concern she cannot carry a baby at all."

Jake felt his blood start to simmer. "And let me guess…that makes her a useless piece of meat to you people."

Roger said nothing. He only turned and walked,

stopping near the door. "We'll see what the tests show." He slipped out the door.

A minute later, as Roger's car sped away up the drive, the group of three lab-coated men carried a sedated Ariel on a stretcher through the doorway.

Jake asked the more official-looking man with the clipboard under his arm, "Where are you taking her?" But he knew the answer. And the man didn't even so much as look at him, they just kept moving through the wide doorway.

Attempting to follow, Jake hurried up to the white van, but was met with a stern straight-arm from the clipboard man holding the van door open.

"Hey!" Jake bounced back. "Get your hands off me."

The man opened his jacket to make sure Jake saw the pistol on his hip. "Don't even try me," he asserted.

Jake took a step back, with every intention of letting this go. But then something came over him. He knew in his heart that if he let them go, he'd never see Ariel again, and he and Ashley would be dead. He charged the man, slamming into him as hard as he could and crushing his body into the van.

The van rocked, propelling them both away from the white vehicle. Jake had no idea what had happened, but in a flash, he was twisted, yanked, and slammed to the concrete surface. Before he could even move, a stiff boot found his chest just below his chin. He lifted his gaze to see the smiling man.

"You're out of your league, punk. You probably thought I was some stuffy doctor. I was a

Goddamned Navy Seal." The man reached into his pocket and pulled out a silencer. With the calmness of a trained killer, he threaded the silencer onto the end of the black pistol then leveled it on Jake's head. "Say goodnight, pumpkin."

"I don't think so!" Ashley said from the doorway to the pool. "Let him up."

The man laughed. "Sure thing, sweetness." He quickly moved, putting the gun on Ashley.

Jake twisted the man's leg hard as gunshots erupted. The man fell and Jake rolled away and popped up to his feet to come face-to-face with the smoking gun in Ashley's hands. He stepped to the side as he realized she was moving toward the van.

Jake bent and snatched up the loose gun on the ground.

"On the ground!" Ashley yelled to the other two men standing with their hands up.

They looked around, confused, then finally started, one-by-one, to sink to their knees and get on the ground. Jake quickly closed the van doors and hurried to the driver's seat.

The second the engine fired, he slammed the shifter into drive and tore away up the driveway, glancing once in the rearview mirror to see the men in the white lab coats were climbing to their feet.

"Where'd you get that gun?" Jake asked.

"It's Mike's…well, it was Mike's."

"You're getting a little too used to shooting people."

"The first one was the hardest."

"I don't know if that makes me feel any better."

"It was life or death, Jake."

"I'm not judging you. What're we doing?"

Ashley huffed. "You're asking me? I have no idea here, Jake. This is your circus to conduct. I've just been following your lead this whole demented trip into the Twilight Zone."

"Playing the hired-gun role apparently." Jake cut the wheel, and with a screech of the tires, headed toward Fort Fisher.

"What's happening?" Ariel called groggily from behind them.

Jake looked up at the mirror but couldn't see her. "Ariel, we're getting you to the ocean."

Chapter 37

After getting Ariel into the water, they stood above the surface looking down at her. She bobbed softly in the gentle surf. "What will I do?"

"You have to get out of here, Ariel," Jake insisted as he looked around nervously.

"Where will I go? How will I eat? I can't get to my garden."

Jake hadn't considered this conundrum. She was not a wild animal. She could not simply be set free into the ocean the way he'd thought.

Ashley touched his arm. Without words, she understood. He met her soft brown eyes. She smiled and gave a subtle nod, "Where would we go?" and he knew.

"The Palladium?"

Ashley shrugged. "Yeah, I mean…"

Jake directed his attention back to Ariel. "Do you know where Harper's Inlet is?"

Ariel narrowed her eyes. "I'm not sure."

"The jetty down by the old docks on the river side, do you know where that jetty leads if you follow the sandbar?"

She nodded. "Yes, I think so."

"At the edge of Harper's Inlet there's an old building. It used to be Palladium Surf Shop many years ago. It was wrecked in a hurricane, but the concrete structure still stands today, and there's a huge basin that flooded into the basement. Go there. There's plenty of places to hide out and we can get you food at nightfall."

Ariel cracked a slight smile. "Okay, I'll do it."

"We'll be there as soon as we can."

Ariel ducked into the surf and splashed away with a kick of her tail.

Ashley let out a long sigh. "Did we do the right thing?"

"Ash, we did the only thing. What other options are there?"

"You tell me."

Jake shook his head. "I'm not sure." He could not help but feel like they'd made some sort of miscalculation. They couldn't just let those people take her.

He started to get a sense of doom.

They took two steps back toward the van when the thumping blades of a helicopter split the morning skies above Fort Fisher. Cracking the wind around them, the rotors thumped in waves.

Jake grabbed Ashley's hand and pulled her quickly toward the van. The chopper swung low, swooping between them and the van. They stopped as the door of the black machine swung open. A man with a large caliber gun waited behind mirrored goggles.

Jake was sure this was it. Death had finally snared them in its clawed trap. But in a flash, the chopper lifted up and gunshots erupted with thunderous violence, slamming into the van instead of their bodies. The van gasped and jerked in mechanical agony as the bullets virtually ripped it apart until it burst into smoke and flames.

They ran off in the other direction, trying desperately to get some distance between them and the death machine in the sky that was clearly set to destroy them. The only shelter was clear across the street in the form of the bunkers of Fort Fisher. He dropped Ashley's hand in order for both of them to run as fast as possible. He felt like his legs would not drive him forward fast enough through the sand.

The roar of the helicopter raged at their backs. He felt a moment of doom just as they got to more solid ground and the firm dirt propelled them forward twice as quickly as they had been moving.

As they approached the paved street, a white van flew toward them, cutting off their path to the safety of Fort Fisher and the shelter. Another van sped in from the other direction. They were boxed in on three sides and that's when Jake realized it was all but over.

A gang of men jumped from the van and began spraying them with gunfire. Jake screamed as he watched bullets tear into Ashley's body. He prayed the bullets would take him, kill his vision. He fell to the ground and screamed as the bullets hit him with wicked force. Only after a moment did he realize his screaming was the only sound. He looked up. As if by magic, everything was gone.

The speeding vans were gone, the helicopter was gone, and the van they drove in was completely intact, as if nothing had ever happened. And most importantly Ashley was fine. Jake was sure he'd died, but the look on Ashley's face was as twisted and confused as his.

As she caught her breath, she huffed, "What the…?"

Jake looked around suspiciously, waiting for the chopper to reappear. "This can't be."

Ashley moved back toward the sand in a few frantic steps. "Are we going insane?"

"We imagined the entire thing?"

"How? How can two people have identical elaborate hallucinations?"

Jake realized he was bleeding from the mouth. He'd bitten is cheek so hard that it took a chunk out. "I don't know what just happened." Jake took a few steps over toward the van, but then hurried back toward the street. He didn't know what to do next. Things were happening in a strange way, the world was shifting. The clouds in the sky moved oddly.

Ashley started speaking to him but her words were broken and garbled. He didn't know if it was her speech or his hearing. She faced him and took a step to square him up.

"Jake, are you okay?" Her words cleared.

He nodded. "I think so."

"What happened?"

"I don't know, but we have to get over to the island."

"Huh? What island?"

"Where we told Ariel to meet us."

"You told her to meet us at the surf shop."

He shook his head. "No, that's not right."

"Yeah, Jake, that's what you said."

He was so confused. "Are you sure?"

She squinted and looked out toward the ocean. "I'm sure. I mean, I think so."

"Ash, we are messed up." Jake didn't know how he knew, but he felt like he'd been drugged or something.

"We were just..." She trailed off and started marching toward the ocean.

Jake watched her for a few long seconds and didn't think much of it, until she started marching straight into the surf.

"Ashley!" He broke into a fast walk, because he could not run. In fact, he was having trouble walking in the right direction. He staggered. The sand seemed to be getting so deep it was sucking him in. It was growing deeper with each step.

Meanwhile Ashley was getting deeper into the water. He could see her just about disappearing into the dark green waves. She was marching to her death and he could not stop her from doing it. He screamed, digging as hard as he could with his legs, trying with desperation to move forward, but he just could not get there.

He watched Ashley's head disappear under the waves and she didn't pop back up.

"Ashley! Ashley!" Jake was just about to give up when his feet suddenly pulled him forward, toward the harder sand near the break. He bolted into the water after her and just slammed into the first set of waves.

After a few seconds, he cleared his vision and looked around. He didn't see her anywhere, but then he felt something hit his midsection and he reached down, catching hold of a hand.

He pulled back toward the shore and Ashley popped up on top of him, gasping what must have been her first breath in a minute. Jake swam backwards a few steps until he was able to catch his heels into the sand and walk back to solid ground.

He collapsed onto the beach with Ashley next to him. Maybe it was the excitement or maybe it was the cool water, but his head finally felt clear. Rolling to face Ashley, he gasped, "Are you okay?"

She wiped some sand off her face. "I'm okay now."

"We have to get out of here."

"We have to get away from that van."

Jake looked at her. "What makes you think it's the van?"

Flopping onto her back, laugh-salted words burst out of her. "I don't know."

It made sense. That van was their van, maybe there was something in it that could cause hallucinations. The problem was, he didn't know when the hallucinations started. "You might be right."

"I feel fine now." She sat up.

Jake levered himself to his feet and held out a hand to Ashley. "Let's get out of here."

"To where?"

"Anywhere, let's just walk." He pulled her up. "I just want to get away from this part of the beach. Something here isn't right."

As usual, she was on the same page of his brain. "When did the hallucination start?"

Jake shrugged. "I don't know." He traced back in his mind. "But as usual we were thinking the same thing."

"Why does that surprise you?"

"Ashley, that's always going to surprise me."

Chapter 38

They reached the back of the house. Jake walked up to the deck and turned to Ashley. "Sam is a little eccentric, but he's cool—he won't ask any questions."

They climbed up the weathered steps, past a dilapidated old doghouse, and to the dirty screen door. Jake knocked on the wooden edge, five sharp raps. "Sammy!"

A thin, middle-aged man, with bad teeth and leathered skin too tan for its own good, came into view. "Jake, y-you salty dog, w-where ya been?" Sam ripped open the flimsy door and gave Jake a one-armed hug. "Haven't seen y-you out in a w-while."

"I've been around. I see the stutter is back."

"Y-yeah only a few w-words. Mostly anything that begins with W and Y."

"Sam, this is Ashley."

He extended a hand. "Fine to meet y-you, pretty lady." He looked her over. "W-what's a beautiful gal like y-you doing w—w-with this beach rat?"

"Sam," Jake interrupted. "I don't have a lot of time, but I need a favor."

Sam's face turned serious. "Sure, kid, name it."

"I need a vehicle, preferably something Jeep-like."

Sam gestured. "Okay, follow."

They walked around to the front of the house through some tall grass, to what looked like a scattered used car lot. There were no less than twelve different vehicles, ranging from old sports cars, to large trucks and SUVs.

"Wow," Jake said. "The collection has grown and shrunk."

"Y-yeah." Sam nodded. "I can't stop buying them. I sold the old Ford pickup, and the two Dodge wagons. But got a nice Spitfire over there and check out by the garage." He pointed to a yellow and black sports machine. "1970 Mustang Mach One."

"Wow," Jake said. "That's in nice shape."

"All original, needs some tuning up and a new interior, but otherwise she's a beautiful runner. Seventy-five-thousand original miles."

Jake eyed a red Ford Bronco. "What about that?"

Sam nodded. "Nineteen-ninety Bronco, she's a runner, got the big V8 and the four-wheel drive works great. She's a beast."

"That's just what I need. I'm going off-road."

Sam nodded. "She's y-your horse. Keys are in it, and I'll tell you what. Give me your bike and she's y-yours forever."

Jake looked at him, and thought about it for a second. "Umm…"

"Ha, just kidding, man. I know y-you love that

bike. But all jokes aside, you like that Bronco, I'll give it to ya cheap."

Jake nodded. "I'll let you know."

Sam pointed a finger. "She's all y-yours. Keep her as long as ya need."

"Thanks, Sam. I really appreciate it."

"No w-worries, kid, but remember, you break her, you bought her." He turned away.

Jake headed over to the jacked-up Ford. Ashley quickly sidled up to him. "That was easy."

"Just like that."

"Nice guy."

"He is, just don't get on his bad side. He's a rattlesnake when he's wronged."

"Well, let's not wrong him."

"Wouldn't dream of it."

They climbed in and Jake fired up the beast. It was big and somewhat burly looking, but it ran smooth and quiet. Jake half expected a big loud exhaust system, but nothing of the sort issued out of the tailpipes. It was just the soft rumble of a V8 engine. And with the soft thump, the truck was in gear and rolling down the unpaved dirt road that led to the main road.

"Where're we going?" Ashley asked as she fished for the seatbelt anchor.

"Well, if any part of this day has been real, we told Ariel to go to the old surf shop. We need to check if she's there."

* * *

Jake navigated the lumpy sand road slowly.

Darkness was setting down on the ocean like a blanket, and even the formidable lights of the Bronco were no match for the abyss that lay ahead of them.

"Jake, I don't like this."

"Neither do I. But it's just up here around this clearing."

When they came to a clearing, the headlights illuminated the side of an old concrete and brick structure. The Palladium Surf Shop was the premier shop at one time in the area, but after a major hurricane washed away the road and half the building, the owners never rebuilt. Eventually the property was annexed back to the town and part of the protected wetlands. Over time it became a place transients set up house, only to learn the dangers of high tide season.

"I'm not sure this was a good idea." Ashley could not hide the worry in her voice and Jake began to feel the same.

He killed the engine but left the lights on.

Stepping out of the truck, their feet were quieted by the sand and the silence was eerie. Only the soft lapping of waves against concrete and deep whirr of the far off heavier waves kept the night alive.

They made their way silently toward the standing remains of the building, hoping to find Ariel where he'd told her to go.

As they reached the gaping hole in the side of the concrete and looked inside, he saw her face, softly lighted by the beams of light. The same twinkle in her eye had always been there but it looked a little less innocent now.

"Ariel," Jake said, "you okay?"

She nodded. "I'm okay."

"Did anyone see you?"

She shook her head. "I don't think so. There was no one around."

Ashley raised her nose into the air. "Do you smell that?"

Jake looked at her. "Smell what?"

"Smells like ozone, like rain, only stronger."

"It's not supposed to rain." Jake said, looking at the clear sky. But he did smell it, it was an odd smell. It smelled like ozone with a hint of burning plastic. He looked back to Ariel. Her smile was not quite as bright as it used to be. "Are you sure you're okay?"

She nodded. "I just have a weird feeling. Maybe I'm just worried."

"I know."

The lights on the Bronco went out and they were plunged into complete darkness except for the moonlight.

"What happened?" Ashley grabbed his arm.

"I don't…" Out over the water, Jake spotted two glowing orange balls of light. He stepped around the building into the clear to get a look. They seemed to be far out over the ocean, maybe a mile, maybe ten miles, it was impossible to say.

"What are they?" Ashley moved up next to him.

He had no answer, but they were definitely coming closer…maybe. Then the two were joined by a third and a fourth, and fifth and sixth, and then two went away, seemingly falling into the water.

"Jake?" Ariel called from the building. When he

didn't answer her, he could hear her splashing her way out of the basement and back into the channel and open waters, following them along the sand.

Jake hadn't even realized that he'd moved so far down the sand, away from the inlet and almost to the beach area that looked out over the open ocean. But the lights were mesmerizing.

None of them realized that the lights had gotten so close. They were just a few hundred feet away but had seemingly not grown in size at all. They still appeared distant.

Then there was a brief flash of light and somehow, a tall woman was standing with them. "They're beautiful," she said in a strange, almost tinny voice.

Jake stopped in his tracks. She was tall, very tall, probably six-foot-three, and very thin. Jake was too stunned to talk, evidently so was Ashley.

The woman motioned her long arm toward the lights. "If you look at them long enough you can see all the mysteries of the Universe right before your eyes."

Jake swallowed. "Where did you...who—are you?"

"I'm a friend, Jake. But we've come to the end of our time here. It is time to put this to rest."

"What—who...where did you come from?" Jake managed to get out. He glanced at Ashley, who was caught between being mesmerized by the orange orbs and the freakishly tall and slender woman that stood with them.

The woman looked up. "I am Avaroush."

"What does that mean?" Jake asked, slowly

losing his inability to think.

"It is a name, like your names, Jake and Ashley, and my Ariel."

Jake looked at Ariel, lying in the shadows of the moon. "Your Ariel?"

"Yes, Jake, she is mine. She belongs to me."

"What? You can't own a person."

Avaroush smiled. "You can if you created her."

"Huh?" He looked at Ashley, both she and Ariel seemed to be in some sort of transfixed state, alert only to the lights in the sky. "What have you done to them?"

"I've done nothing. They are in full control of themselves. They're choosing to notice what they want to notice."

"They look…" He reached out and touched Ashley. "Hey, can you hear me?"

Ashley nodded. "Yes."

Jake looked back to the lights. "What are they?"

"They've come for my Ariel. We must leave now."

"I don't understand."

"You may never understand, Jake, and that's okay. Not all things are meant to be understood before their time."

"Please, I want to understand. I need to understand."

"What is it that you need to understand?"

"Is this real?"

"Is what real?"

"You tell me. I mean, is Ariel a mermaid? Was she made in a lab? Is she a human?"

"Sometimes the answers you get are not the truth

you were seeking. Sometimes things are put in place to give them the illusion of reality, or the reality of illusion. You were shown what you needed to be shown and only that. What makes you so special is that you still cared."

"You're not making sense."

"But it all makes sense, Jake. It all has some truth and it all has some lie. You seek the truth you want to fit the narrative you believe."

"I don't understand."

"You will."

"Am I dreaming?"

"No, you are not dreaming."

"What has happened? What part is real? Which reality is the truth?"

"Everything is truth. Everything is real, Jake. All the magic in the world is reality. It is only when you stop believing that it becomes unreal. Age and wisdom bring with it a fleeting grip on the magic of the universe. It falls through your fingers, as do the molecules of time."

"I'm dead, aren't I?" Jake had a gut-wrenching feeling that he was dead, that he'd pulled that trigger after all, and none of this was real. He died on those rocks just down a ways from where he stood now. That everything had, in fact, been a dream, and had come full circle. And now this weird woman was going to snap her fingers and end the dream-slash-nightmare.

"We are all alive and dead at different times, Jake. What we choose to believe is our reality in that moment, in that dimension, in that Universe. We exist and do not exist simultaneously. We are both mortal and immortal. We awake from every dream into a new dream, from every life into a new life, and realities are fluid and evolving and multi-dimensional."

"I don't know what you're saying."

"Yes, you do know. Look into the magic of your heart and you will see all the truth you need. You will never see more truth than you do right now."

Jake closed his eyes, and suddenly everything seemed perfect, everything made sense. He smiled and nodded. "I think maybe I understand."

"Jake, you are special. We chose you, to save you, because you need to be the one who keeps our legend alive. You have the wonder. You have the magic inside. But you are young, and you are not ready for that responsibility. We ask of you only one thing. Don't let the magic inside you die."

"I'll try."

"We will return in time, and you will be ready. But until then we must take our leave of this place."

The lights were now close enough to feel their heat. Jake caught his breath.

"It is time to say goodbye now."

"I must know one thing."

"Yes?"

"Is Ariel going to die?"

She smiled. "No, legends do not die, they just go home."

"Now, please say your goodbye."

Jake went over to Ariel and bent to her in the sand. He kissed her on the forehead. "Goodbye, Ariel. I will never forget you."

Ariel smiled. "I'll see you again soon."

Then in a blinding flash of orange light, she was gone.

Jake stood up, looked back to where Avaroush stood, and she too was gone, the orange lights were gone. Ashley was there, and that was all that mattered.

Chapter 39

Jake sat alone on the bench, looking at the ocean at Fort Fisher. He still liked to come here from time to time, although he'd nearly given up hope that Ariel would return. Maybe someday she would. Actually, he knew in his heart that she would. Even if she didn't, he knew in some way she'd always be with him, even if he never saw her again. Just like Cassie. They were both forever a part of him, embedded in a special place of his heart.

He glanced at his watch and realized it was almost time to meet Ashley at Carolina Beach. They were meeting with the reverend who would be officiating their wedding. Jake had asked her to marry him on the one year anniversary of the night he'd first seen Ariel. Not because he'd seen her, but because that was the night his new life officially started and his old one officially died.

He still had some sneaking suspicious feeling that maybe his life did end that night, and this was the new reality he'd created. After all, anything is possible and life is impossible.

Meeting Ariel had changed his life, for the worse and for the better. He'd learned a lot since that night, but the most important thing was to treasure every moment we have here in this Earth, in this reality. He knew that someday, a part of Ariel would return to this beach. After all, legends never die. They only take a break until someone once again believes in magic.

Acknowledgements

I would like to thank my fans, who have had a great deal of patience with me while I rebooted my life and took a couple years away from writing. It's been a wild couple of years but I'm back and ready to keep the thrills coming.

I would also like to thank the team at Limitless Publishing for their unending support and dedication.

As always, most of all, I want to thank my friends and family. Without all of you, I would not be where I am today.

Special thanks to Toni "Blankenscraggins" for allowing me to crash into her life and bust everything in sight. I love you for all the things.

About the Author

Shane Scollins is an Amazon best selling author who grew up in Northern New Jersey. After spending over a decade in the snowy mountains of Upstate New York, he has since relocated to the beaches of Wilmington, NC. Primarily a suspense/thriller writer, Shane enjoys taking readers on surprising and unexpected journeys that sometimes venture into the paranormal/supernatural. He is currently working on his next book.

Facebook:
https://www.facebook.com/pages/Shane-Scollins-Author/208046712568634

Twitter:
https://twitter.com/shanescollins

Website:
http://www.shanescollins.com/

Goodreads:
http://www.goodreads.com/author/show/4893553.Shane_Scollins